THE WAY
Of The Sun

Mike Ike Chinwuba

Grosvenor House
Publishing Limited

The right of Mike Ike Chinwuba to be identified as the author of this
work has been asserted by him in accordance with Section 78
of the Copyright, Designs and Patents Act 1988

The book cover picture is copyright to Inmagine Corp LLC

This book is published by
Grosvenor House Publishing Ltd
28-30 High Street, Guildford, Surrey, GU1 3EL.
www.grosvenorhousepublishing.co.uk

A CIP record for this book
is available from the British Library

ISBN 978-1-78148-689-4

Chapter 1

It is just before noon on a summer's day. The weather is kind but the clouds intermittently struggle to restrict the sun from emerging fully. Morris, a young man of about forty-five, decides to clean out his car. The car is parked in the street just by his house, the car radio is on and Morris is enthusiastically cleaning the car's floor as he sings along with the music.

Suddenly, he hears a very faint and feeble voice calling, "young man", to which he pays no attention. Perhaps he does not feel he is young enough to be referred to in this way. As he carries on with the cleaning, the same voice resounds again: "young man" still faint and feeble. This time he hesitantly stops and gradually looks up in the direction of the pavement, by the side of his car, and there is this very elderly lady with a walking stick leaning against a hedge and looking sternly at him. He gazes at her for a moment with apparent surprise and puts his cleaning stuff aside. Approaching the lady, he exudes a lightening kind of smile.

"Hello, and how are you?" he asks. He notices some relief in the lady's face and a certain sense of accomplishment. Could it be because he gave her such a bewildering and pleasant response which she did not expect?

He leans against his car with his hands folded over his chest.

"Do you live in this neighbourhood, young man?" she asks.

"Yes," Morris replies, pointing to a house in the corner of the street. "That's my house over there."

The elderly lady notices that Morris is quite relaxed and not perturbed by interruption from cleaning his car. It is obvious that he wants to give her his full attention and time; she seems delighted. Nevertheless, she wants to kill time and he is prepared to let her.

I have seen you on occasions getting out of your car or driving off, but you always seem to be jolly and full of energy. In this age of austerity, money is quite tight and no-one cares about anyone, I guess it is strictly time for self-preservation, no more and no less." says the elderly lady.

"Thank you, replies Morris, "I just tend to stay calm and carry on with life, irrespective of circumstances. I learnt from experience that circumstances do not change because I want them to, they change through perseverance and taking actions to change them. So, I just give it a good crack and hope for the best."

"I wish everyone had your philosophy, young man."

Suddenly, she positions her walking stick on the pavement and detaches herself from the hedge and starts to walk away, turning to Morris.

"Thank you for your time young man, I must head to the shop."

"No worries", replies Morris.

Morris goes back in his car and starts to clean it, but not with the same enthusiasm as before. A good forty minutes must have past and he still does not know whether the lady lives in the street, is a neighbour or whatever. He did not ask. Nevertheless, he's pleased that he gave her his time. Consequently, a lot of differing thoughts continually occur in his mind. He wonders whether she has grandchildren; does she live alone; if she had sons or daughters or even grandchildren, or great-grandchildren, why would she be going to the shops on her own? If she lives by herself, why don't the social services provide her with a care assistant? It certainly seems that the brief encounter has triggered such a deep compassionate concern.

Three weeks' later...

It is Friday evening. Morris decides to get his car cleaned. On Saturday he will be meeting up with friends to socialise. The weather is still in the grip of summer, so he fills a bucket with water and goes outside to the road where his car is parked. As usual, he turns his car radio on and starts singing along while he cleans the car. He is bending down, cleaning the tyres when suddenly he hears a familiar voice -

"Young man." The voice is faint and feeble. Morris stops cleaning, he looks up and is astonished to see the same elderly lady whom he met the last time he cleaned his car. She is immaculately dressed in a flowery dress and each strand of her hair is in the right place. Although, it is hot and summery, she is wearing a scarf round her neck. She is leaning against a hedge with the support of her walking stick. However, Morris is astonished in seeing the same lady in the same circumstances, but this time around there is no hesitation. He stops what he was doing and approaches her in the same manner as he did last time.

Morris asks, "Did you get everything you required from the shop?"

"Young man, just being able to get to the shops and look around is a delightful accomplishment, even when I do not purchase anything," the elderly lady replies, as she looks at Morris as though she anticipates some comment or at least a question, but he is playing a good listener and is just nodding in agreement. She continues, "When one is lying in bed all day and all night, one needs to get out and about." Morris is listening with a compassionate expression.

"Have you got a family young man?" She asks.

"Yes." Replies Morris.

"It's nice to have a family." She says.

She sighs with a deep sense of regret. Detaching herself from the hedge she starts to walk away.

"It is nice to see you again, young man, must not distract you from your work." She says.

Morris is still standing on the spot, watching her as the elderly lady walks to the bottom of the road. She stops near a telephone box apparently waiting to go in and make a call but a man is inside the phone box using the phone. She is still waiting and Morris is watching from a distance. It seems that she is getting impatient as the man in the phone box has stayed too long.

Suddenly, she angrily staggers to the phone box, opens the door, furiously drags the man out, closes the door behind her and starts making a call. The man is now standing outside the phone box gasping with fright. After a while, he makes a quick getaway, increasing his steps as he disappears in the distance. Morris is astonished and returns to his car and continues cleaning.

4

The following day...

It is late morning and Morris is sitting in his lounge, talking on the telephone. There is a knock on the front door; the knock is weak and indecisive. He ignores it as he is not expecting anyone and does not answer the door to sales people. There is another knock, this time it is persistent but still weak. So he hurries to the front door and opens it. To his amazement, the elderly lady is standing right in front of it, supporting herself with a walking stick.

"Hello, nice to see you. Please come in," says Morris.

"Not today thank you," she replies, she opens her handbag and rummaging inside it for a while she produces a set of keys and emphatically holds them out to him.

"My house keys, my house number is fifty-one. It is for you to enter as you please and sort out my letters for me when they arrive in the post, and also to collect my prescriptions from my doctor and send them to me fortnightly." She forcibly puts the keys into Morris's hand. "I trust you!" She exclaims.

Morris is instantly dazed as he clutches the keys. He is staring at her with combined expressions of shock, bewilderment and fear.

She adds, "I will be going on holiday to Israel."

"When"? Morris asks.

"This afternoon" Replies the elderly lady.

"Alone" Enquires Morris.

"Yes, from Gatwick Airport" – says the elderly lady.

"How are you getting to the airport?" asks Morris.

"By train," she replies.

There is silence. Morris wonders how this elderly lady could get to the airport by herself when she is finding it very difficult to walk, or stand unsupported; let alone ascend and descend the stairs at the underground stations to the airport.

"When you are ready to go let me know and I will drop you off," says Morris.

The elderly lady is delighted.

"Oh, will you? That's very kind."

She abruptly turns around and walks away.

He does not know her name or where she lives and hardly knew anything about her, and here he is, holding her entire house keys in his hand.

However, she seems determined, but nevertheless, quite vulnerable and helpless but he is prepared to do his best for her. Morris goes back in his lounge and makes phone calls to cancel some of the arrangements he had made with his friends. He does not think he would be able to keep them since he does not know when he would be back from the airport.

Fifty minutes have passed since the elderly lady left, and then there is a knock at the front door. He hurries and opens it and it is the elderly lady again; she returns this time wheeling a small suitcase.

"Give me a minute, I will get the car keys," says Morris.

He goes into his lounge, a couple of minutes later he comes out again with the car keys.

He is tucking his shirt into his jeans and locking his front door at the same time. As they drive to the airport there is a stunned silence between them, and Morris is gradually becoming uncomfortable. He is wondering, who could she be visiting in Israel and for what purpose? At this point, Morris is determined to find out and turns

6

to the elderly lady to ask questions, only to find she has dosed off. It is sort of mixed feeling for Morris because on the one hand, he is quite relieved of the torture of the silence, yet on the other hand, he may not satisfy his curiosity by not solving the mystery that has been bugging his mind. As he continues driving, he is wondering if the golden moment would expire – if it does, it means that he has to wait until her return from Israel in order to find out who she was going to Israel to meet and why, considering she is well-advanced in age and should not be travelling alone.

The sun is slowly peering through the windscreen.

Suddenly, the elderly lady says, "We have not got to the airport yet."

"Oh! We will be there in a few minutes," replies Morris.

The elderly lady lowers the sun screen and laughs out loud. Morris glances at her in silent wonder.

"What is the matter?" asks Morris.

"I was dreaming about my friend – Isabella, my Jewish friend. We worked together during the war, for the Russians and the British as double agents. She can speak fluent Russian in addition to three other languages. After the war, we were strolling along a river bank around 2am, at full moon, when suddenly we noticed an aeroplane flying overhead – quite low indeed. So, we stood still wondering what could be amiss. As it reached the middle of the river, it started to hover around. As it went round and round, the tail end opened and a lot of stuff was dumped on to the river and then it flew away into the dark side of the moon and vanished."

She glances questioningly at Morris. "Yes, the dark side of the moon." She says.

"The spot where we were standing was on the boundary between night and day. So, we were in the 'night' side of the divide, but about three hundred metres in the opposite direction, it was day; in other words, 'light'. From our experiences, we realised that whatever it was that was dumped had to be dangerous or illegal. During the war, we would stand around that spot watching the Russian soldiers loading stuff into Land Rovers." She takes a quick glance at Morris.

"You know what I mean? Loading ammunition for the war across the border. It was an excellent environment for espionage."

For a while, there is silence. Morris is speechless as differing thoughts keep running wild in his mind. Suddenly, the elderly lady bursts into laughter and then she sighs.

"Do you know, what was dumped in that river was a large quantity of nuclear waste."

Chapter 2

They arrive at the airport terminal; Morris pulls up along the passenger drop-off bay. Standing graciously on the pavement is a young and beautiful lady, sartorially dressed. She is talking into her mobile phone.

As she catches their eyes, the elderly lady says to Morris with a smile, "Isn't she beautiful," she is referring to the young lady.

Morris, with a nod of approval says, "Yes, she is indeed."

Morris gets out of the car and opens the side door, enabling the old lady to step out, she then proceeds towards the young lady. Morris retrieves the small suitcase for the elderly lady to collect. He notices that she is casually chatting with the young lady, so he leans on the car and waits. No sooner does he start getting a little impatient than the elderly lady starts returning to the car with the young lady. As they approach the car, the elderly lady introduces Henrietta.

"Morris, this beautiful young lady is called Henrietta and I want you to drive her to Wimbledon". Then she turns to Henrietta and says, "this is Morris, I find him a selfless young man and he is forthright, you have nothing to fear. He will look after you."

The elderly lady collects her suitcase and gives Morris a piece of paper:

"This is where I will be staying in Israel. Send my medicines there," she says. She gives Morris a cheeky wink and walks off with the help of her walking stick into the departure lounge.

Morris was about to help Henrietta into the car but she opens the front passenger's door cheerily and gets in. She is quite relaxed and unperturbed. Morris then gets in and drives off.

"So you live in Wimbledon", Asks Morris

"No," replies Henrietta.

"Staying in Wimbledon?"

"No,"

"Meeting someone"?

"No," replies Henrietta.

Morris becomes anxious, their eyes meet and they erupt in laughter.

So, Morris asks emphatically, "why are you going to Wimbledon?"

Henrietta replies, "Just looking for somewhere to live and then I saw an advertisement on the website for a flat to let, - so I am going to see the flat. Does that make sense?"

Morris recaps, "so, you are looking for somewhere to live ...right?"

Henrietta says "Yes".

Morris continues, "And you saw an advertisement on a website ....right?"

"Right", replies Henrietta.

"And you are going to view the flat." Says Morris.

With a nod of the head, Henrietta says, "Sure".

There is a pause as she glances at Morris and smiles.

Henrietta asks Morris "Do you know, you have a very kind face and you are also positively very funny?"

"Is that right?" asks Morris

"Yes, have you not been told that before?" Asks Henrietta.

Morris says, "I don't remember, but a classic one was that I went into a Chinese takeaway, the Chinese man, as soon as he saw me stared at me for a while and yelled, 'Nelson Mandela!!'

Henrietta asks inquisitively, "Was he referring to you?"

"Yes," Morris continues, "with a smile and excitement all over his face. Then he called his colleague who was busy in the kitchen to come and witness. His colleague was motionless as soon as he saw me. They were quite pleasant and excitable. They emphasised that Nelson Mandela must have looked exactly like me when he was young."

Henrietta anxiously asks, "And then what happened?"

"I was served a generous portion of rice and chicken chow-mein. Since then they have become my fans. Very kind and harmless young men". Replies Morris.

"Quite an experience," Henrietta affirms.

"Interesting experience," says Morris.

"She is quite funny and exciting is she not?" Henrietta asks enquiringly.

"Who?" asks Morris.

"The elderly lady that you dropped off." Says Henrietta.

"Oh yes, Intriguing and charismatic", replies Morris.

"Who is she?" asks Henrietta.

"Good question. I do not know" replies Morris.

Henrietta is a little startled but does not display apparent uneasiness.

"What!?" Henrietta yells. "She referred to you as her son."

"Do you know, every old lady or old man that I meet calls me 'son', so it is not strange to me." Says Morris.

"Obviously, I knew you were not her son; you couldn't have been, unless you were adopted by her. I mean, she is Russian and you are…?"

"African," replies Morris.

Henrietta acknowledges, "So, two different shades of black and white. How did you two meet?"

Morris replies, "She said 'hello' to me twice and then the third time she rang my door bell; resulting in me having to drop her off at the airport".

"Really!?" Exclaims Henrietta.

Morris replies, "Yes. Well, not exactly, but something like that".

"Do you see what I mean… you have a kind face and people see that, just make sure that it is not exploited". She warns.

Morris says, "I can never be exploited, given the law of averages, one may take advantage just once and no more".

"How do you mean"? Henrietta asks

"Truth sticks out like a sore thumb. When I see that someone honestly needs help, I do not hesitate to try and do what I can to help," says Morris.

"Why?" Asks Henrietta.

"Cause everyone needs some help sometimes, and I mean everyone".

"So you mean to save the world single handed?"

Morris replies, "I wish I could but that's not what I mean. Imagine one person helping just one other person and that other person helps another person and so on; inevitably the whole world will benefit from the compassion or the revolution of a single mind. Obviously, the desire to help should arise from a change in the depths of one's life to make a difference. This is a revolution in one's life, so in consequence the whole world will change. In this world of greed, anger and foolishness, it seems that everyone is for himself or herself and no one cares how one tries to dominate or wants to be better than Mr and Mrs Jones next door. Consequently, there are some who will suffer in this quagmire. The people who pay the price for this inadequacy and selfishness are the weak. These weak ones in turn rise against the poisons in form of rebellion and anarchy doing harm to others. It goes in cycles...which result in more chaos, suffering and insecurity for all. Ordinary people in turn rise against their leaders. We can all see it happening right now in most countries. It is clearly evident. What is required to cleanse this society is immense compassion, which, in turn, breeds security and modesty."

Henrietta, who has been listening attentively, gives a conscious sigh of agreement.

"One thing that you have not considered in your well-thought-out philosophy is that not everyone is rich enough to help others. If one does not have enough money for oneself, how could one help, especially those who have families". Says Henrietta.

She fixes her gaze at Morris as if to say; *how would you deal with that?*

Morris, returns the gaze at Henrietta, and without hesitation he says-

"It's not all about money, everyone has something to share. For example, if a person is hungry, we should give bread. When there is no bread, we can at least give words that nourish. To a person who looks ill or is physically frail, we can turn the conversation to some subject that will lift their spirits and fill them with the hope and determination to get better. We should give something to each person we meet, such as joy, courage, hope, assurance, positive philosophy, wisdom, a vision for the future. Everyone can give something! In such an environment, everyone is a winner because everyone receives and everyone gives – so it is a ceaseless cycle of positive cause and effect".

"cause and effect?" Repeats Henrietta.

"Yes, you have heard of a common saying that what goes around comes around".

"Yes, as you mentioned, it is a common saying".

"Excellent," says Morris. "Good cause is born from compassionate deed and bad cause from bad deed such as greed, anger and stupidity. In a positive cycle the majority of the people are happy and there is not much suffering and hence genuine security is established".

There is silence for a considerable period. Now they have reached Wimbledon. As Morris takes the last turning towards the town centre, there is a long stretch of traffic that prevents them from moving as they are at the tail end of the immobile vehicles. The car-horns are sounding furiously but all the cars are Stationary.

Morris gets out of his car while Henrietta remains inside. As he walks to the front of the traffic, he notices an elderly man and woman standing in front of the car with the bonnet open. Morris approaches them, and speaks to them in a soft voice.

"What seems to be the problem?" Asks Morris.

"We got to this point and the car stalled and then stopped." The elderly man replies.

"And we are causing all this havoc; they have been hooting and swearing instead of trying to help". Says the woman.

Morris reassuring them, "Do not worry. I am here to help you".

"Oh bless you, do you think you can sort it?" Asks the woman.

As Morris begins to fiddle with the cables on the engine,

He replies, "I strongly believe that where there is a will there is always a way".

In Morris's car, Henrietta is getting impatient wondering where Morris has got to. She looks at her watch then gets out of the car and starts to walk in the same direction as Morris. As she walks passed all the cars in the traffic, she notices Morris focusing on the engine of the broken-down car. She approaches Morris, though she is slightly annoyed.

"So this is where you are". Asks Henrietta.

"It won't be long and I will drop you off". Replies Morris

"Don't bother, I will walk. It is not far from here". says Henrietta.

"Okay, call me and let me know how you get on".

As she is walking away, she says, "I don't have your number".

"It's OK, I will call you," he replies

Henrietta asks, "How is that possible when you don't have my number?"

"I will call you", Morris repeats with confidence.

Henrietta walks away hurriedly.

After spending a few more minutes on the engine, Morris requests the man to start the car. He gets in, turns the key and the car starts. By the time Morris has walked back to his car, the traffic has cleared.

However, Morris drives home feeling fulfilled and happy. In one day he has helped an old lady with a lift to the airport, dropped off a lady in Wimbledon and helped fix an old couple's car in a space of about three hours and has not done anything for himself.

As Morris relaxes pondering about the day, he remembers that he does not know anything about Henrietta except that she was looking for a flat to rent.

Chapter 3

It is late evening and Morris refreshes himself and changes his clothes. Anthony, his friend, has just phoned him up and wishes to meet up with him in a restaurant in Wimbledon village. So Morris gets in his old Mercedes car and drives off to meet Anthony. As he gets to the end of his street, which is a "T" junction, he stops for traffic, and suddenly a classic car suddenly pulls up in front of Morris and a middle-aged man, called Mr Knight, gets out of the passenger seat and starts walking towards Morris's car. Morris is wondering what is happening. As Mr Knight gets closer to Morris's car, he starts examining the Mercedes. He goes to the back and has a good look, then at the sides. He goes to the driver's side window where Morris is sitting and knocks on the window. Morris gently presses the electrically controlled button and the window opens.

"How much do you want for this car?" Enquires Mr Knight.

Morris is bewildered at the sudden enthusiasm in his questioning.

"It is not for sale". Replies Morris

Mr Knight insists, "Fine, but how much would you want for it?"

Morris relenting, "Okay, make me an offer".

Mr Knight offers Morris about double the market value of the car.

Morris replies, "That's a reasonable offer but I must say that I do not wish to sell the car now".

The man is now examining the inside of the car which looks immaculately clean and well-preserved. The foot mats are original and stainless. He makes another offer, which is about three times the value of the car.

"May I have your business card so that if I decide to sell it I will give you a call," asks Morris.

"Fair enough," replies Mr Knight.

Mr Knight walks back to his car and confers with a young man sitting in the driver's seat, who opens the glove compartment and hands over a card. Mr Knight then walks over to Morris and gives him the card.

"This is my business card and the man in my car is my son. Please do let me know whenever you intend to sell your car," says Mr Knight.

"Be sure of that. I will let you know first".

Mr Knight walks back to his car and drives off.

Morris is fascinated by the offer because he did not think that his old Mercedes was worth that much. However, he is quite happy.

Morris drives off and wonders why the man wanted his car so desperately that he offered him up to three times the market price of such an old car. Nevertheless, he has now an extraordinary event to communicate to Anthony when he meets him at the Restaurant.

Anthony is an old friend of Morris, he is the only child of wealthy parents who are deceased. As a result, he inherited all his parents' wealth at the age of twenty-five; he is now in his thirties. He has always cherished

Morris's friendship because Morris, out of compassion, has always been there for Anthony whenever he has needed him. He has given him effective advice and protected him from his vulnerability and susceptibility to deceit from false friends who were steeped in greed and ready to relieve him of his money. Morris is an ordinary working man, who is far from being well-to-do, but who has always been vivacious, self-sufficient and happy. He always gives Anthony a lot of valuable time whenever he needs him.

Consequently, Anthony always relies on Morris's advice and companionship. Most of all he feels comfortably secure whenever they are together.

Morris parks his car and enters the restaurant. He looks around for Anthony who has not yet arrived, so he goes to a table in the corner and sits down. He begins to read the menu and Anthony cheerily walks in and joins him at the table.

"What's happened to you, Anthony?" Asks Morris.

"Why?" Says Anthony.

"You seem to be unusually very happy. It is really great to see you like this".

"Quite right my dear friend. Guess what happened today".

"So, what happened?" Asks Morris.

"I met this fine girl a couple of hours ago, she is really dishy".

"No wonder, I should have guessed. Where?"

"Starbucks, by the station".

"Not from this neighbourhood is she?" asks Morris.

"No. From Australia, I walked into Starbucks, grabbed a coffee, and as I looked for a seat I saw this beautiful girl sitting alone sipping a cup of coffee and there is a piece of cake on her table. So, I walked over with my coffee and said 'hello'. She said 'hello' back with a welcoming smile, so I sat down by the same table and next thing I remember – we were having a conversation," says Anthony.

At this time the waitress approaches Morris and Anthony's table, takes their orders and leaves. Anthony continues, telling Morris that the woman he met is a local news reader in Australia but wants to settle in the UK. She has a lovely name too.

Morris asks, "What is her name?"

"Henrietta".

Morris was instantly startled and repeats the name. "Henrietta?"

"Yes," replies Morris, "She is looking for a flat in Wimbledon but the landlord was not available to show her the flat so she came to Starbucks to chill for a while."

"So she did not see the flat?" Morris asks.

Anthony explains, "She has another appointment to view the flat tomorrow. The landlord was a long way away in Dorset and could not get here to organise the viewing. He got stuck in traffic, so he asked her to come tomorrow. One thing though ..."

"What?" Morris asks.

Anthony continues, "She kept on talking about somebody she met on the way to Wimbledon. I think she is in love with this person because she kept on talking about how genuine and selfless he was. She did not stop talking about this guy and for a while and I began to think that it was all a waste of time continuing the conversation. Nevertheless, I succeeded in getting her phone number."

Anthony takes out a piece of paper from his top pocket and puts it on the table. "That's her phone number, I have done well in getting it." He praises himself.

Morris picks up the piece of paper and inputs the number in his mobile phone.

"What do you think you are doing?" asks Anthony.

"Is she wearing purple top and black jeans?" Morris asks.

Anthony is astonished at the perfect description of Henrietta's clothes. His jaws drop.

Anthony replies with astonishment, "Yes, yes! You've done it again. How do you know?"

Anthony's usage of this phrase 'you've done it again' is derived from an experience Morris had about his neighbours a few months back. He and his neighbours have good relationship and they knew his name and always addressed him by his name. On the contrary, Morris did not remember their names and did not address them by their names. He knew it would not be appropriate to ask them what their names were since he has known them for about five years. Morris was not happy about this shortcoming and had been waiting for an opportunity to find out what their names were. So, one morning he went to do his meditation as he always does before going to work. During the meditation the thought of how to find out what their names were crossed his mind, so, he desires to find out.

After the meditation, he went to work. He did not think about it any more. On his return in the evening, he puts his keys in his front door and opens it, and behind the door, there were letters lying on the carpet which the postman had put in his letter box by mistake as none of the letters belonged to Morris. He picked them up, read the names and the addresses on the envelops to find that they belonged to his neighbours. From the names and the house numbers he realised they were for his neighbours. So he went directly to their houses and rang the door bell. As they opened the door he confidently called them by their names and gave them their letters. It was quite profound and mystic because in the morning, he only thought about a way to find out what their names were and by the evening he got the answer without effort.

"I gave her a lift from the airport to Wimbledon today and she talked about going to view a flat", says Morris. "That's the only detail I managed to obtain, and her name of course, because we were introduced."

"Typical! So you are this brilliant guy she did not stop talking about – 'genuine and selfless' as she put it. My God, she is in love with you, really in love". Says Anthony.

"I did not know she felt that way considering that I left her in the traffic jam to help an elderly couple whose car had broken down. I only try to do the right thing moment by moment. It does not really matter if one appreciates or not – just do it." Says Morris.

"Are you going to call her?" Asks Anthony.

"I don't know yet. I did promise to call her but did not have her number" replies Morris.

"How were you going to do that when you do not have her number?"

Morris says, "Through strong belief and power of thought. It is like when the sun appears, darkness is instantly dispelled. When one's life is constantly sustained in that shining realm of life, nothing remains a secret."

"Are you going to call her?" Anthony persists.

"If I do, it won't be for what you have in mind". Replies Morris.

The waitress arrives with their order.

Chapter 4

Few days later, Morris decides to visit the elderly lady's house; she may have some letters that need his attention. He picks up the set of keys which the elderly lady entrusted to him and leaves for number fifty-one.

Number fifty-one is a fairly large house that stands majestically near the end of the street. Two trees of average height stand right in front of it; their branches obscuring the top half of the building.

When Morris opens the front door, he senses a strong smell of dampness so he stands at the door for a while examining the interior that seems to be in a time warp – dark and gothic. The stairs to the right leads upstairs and just at the other side of the beginning of the stairs is a large room on the right hand side. The hall leads directly from the front door to the kitchen, adjacent to the kitchen is a small room which contains a small bed, a chair and a table. An antique telephone is placed by the bedside.

Morris picks up a couple of letters from the front door and proceeding along the hall towards the kitchen, he notices numerous old paintings hanging on the sides of the hallway. The walls are covered with very old wallpaper, which seems to have seen many years. From the looks of the wallpaper, it is apparent that the colours have severely faded.

Morris reaches the small room and enters the kitchen. To his surprise, the kitchen looks as if it hasn't been used for a very long time, He also notices there is no heating appliance whatsoever in the house. From the kitchen window he peers into the garden. The garden is large and well kept, and at the end of the garden is a small make-shift house painted in a variety of colours which do not blend in with its environment. Morris retreats to the front door and examines the two letters he has in his hand. The name reads *Dr A. Bozivich*. On the sender's side, it reads *from the clinic*. It is from the elderly lady's GP, reminding her to collect her prescription. The other letter, which is addressed with the same title, is an invitation from the Russian Embassy for a party.

Morris hurriedly exits the house, closes and locks the front door and walks back to his own house. In his mind he is wondering how the elderly lady has endeavoured to survive many winters without any heating or cooked food. It also crosses his mind that she is in fact a doctor, but does not know if it was a doctor of medicine or a doctorate in a certain field of academia. Whichever it may be, it's a great achievement.

Morris looks at his watch. Without hesitation, he grabs his car keys and the letter from the GP and goes to his car and drives off. He pulls up at the GP's surgery and hand s over the letter to the receptionist. The receptionist is a good-looking young lady and is well-spoken. She asks Morris to take a seat and that he would be called to see the GP. It is obvious that the surgery is busy because many patients are waiting to be seen. The receptionist takes the letter to the GP inside the consultation room. Morris takes a magazine from the table to read when the receptionist returns.

"I have never seen you here before. You are not registered here, are you?" asks Receptionist.

"No, my GP is close to my home so I do not have to travel far to see him." Replies Morris.

Receptionist asks, "Do you live in this neighbourhood?"

"No, but close," Morris replies

"Why don't you register here, many people from afar come to this surgery". Says Receptionist.

Morris looks round the waiting room; full of patients.

"I noticed, because it is really busy here. The point is that I do not see my GP very often, says Morris.

"You must be very fit then. My God you do look fit and healthy," says Receptionist.

"I thank goodness for that but sometimes looking fit does not necessarily mean one is healthy. One may experience a small ailment, and by seeing the GP one averts a major catastrophe. I do remember vividly that the Buddha said that there are four stages that every man or woman, in fact everything in the universe has to go through." Says Morris.

"Like what?" Enquires Receptionist.

By this time the patients in the waiting room are silently but intently listening to the conversation as the receptionist takes particular interest in Morris.

Morris replies, "Birth, old age, sickness and death. These four stages await everyone and everything in our universe."

"Everything?" Asks Receptionist.

"Yes, everything including the sun and the moon. For human beings - it is really a blessing if one is fortunate to go through these stages. However, some of us may not go through all these stages. Some may just get through one or two of these stages and demise. So, if one is born and is fortunate to see old age, that is in itself a blessing and great good fortune." Replies Morris.

At this moment, a male patient joins in the conversation;

"Tell that to the kids of today, even your own children", he sighs, "they write you off when you get old, no respect!"

"Not all of them. Some do and some don't." Says Receptionist.

"Did you say that everything in the universe goes through these stages?"

"Definitely, for human beings, if they are fortunate enough."

"What about cars, clothes or even trees?" Enquires Receptionist.

"Take a car for example, you buy a new car, it works fine and the engine is silent and energetic, then after a few years it starts to develop some problems and it is forever being taken to the mechanic and eventually the parts are worn out or become obsolete and it is resigned to the scrap yard. That is, it dies, and as for clothes..."

"Yes, clothes". Says Receptionist.

Morris says, "You buy new clothing, it looks great and every thread is in the right place, and then you keep washing and maybe ironing it. For a while it is in good shape, but when this process continues for a few months or a few years, it starts to discolour and lose shape, as time goes on it disintegrates. For the trees", continues Morris, "a seed germinates and grows into a big tree and survives for many years, then it starts to deteriorate, stops growing and it begins to shrink and wither and it dies, the sun, the moon and the stars go through the same stages but time span may be longer. Death is a crucial part of life's cycle. The problem is, human being are always afraid to talk about death and also, sometimes about sex. These are the realities of life but we are scared to talk about them.

President Ikeda, the third SGI President, in his reference to a thesis on the philosophy of life, states that "the universe is life itself, and that life, together with the universe, is eternal and everlasting. He said that, 'Just as we sleep and wake and then sleep again, we live and die and live again, maintaining our lives eternally. And when we wake up in the morning, we resume our activities based on the same mind as the previous day, in the same way, in each existence we are destined to live based on the result of the karmic causes created in our previous lives. He also explained that if we liken the universe to an ocean, our lives are like the waves that appear and disappear on the surface of the ocean; the waves and the ocean are not separate entities. In other words, the universe is but part of the ocean's ongoing activity.

As the ocean waves, so the universe 'peoples' – what we therefore see as 'death', empty space or nothingness, is only the trough between the crests of this endless waving ocean of life."

Just at that moment, a patient comes out the consulting room followed by the GP. The GP looks around and observes that the patients in the reception area are all glowing and vibrant as if they have been having a party. So he smiles and says, "Are all of you waiting to see me?"

"They are all here to see you, Doctor." Says Receptionist.

"You all seem to be happy and healthy," says GP

"Not before this young man came in." interrupts Lady Patient.

So the GP turns around and walking back to his consulting room - he calls out, "Morris, in my consulting room please."

Some of the patients are wondering why the GP called Morris first, despite the fact that they all arrived before him. However, they did not complain. They were rather displeased that the extraordinary discussion came to an abrupt end.

Morris follows the doctor into the consulting room. The GP writes a couple of prescriptions and hands them over to Morris.

"Where did you meet Dr. Bozivich?" asks GP.

"In the street," replies Morris.

GP says, "Very uncharacteristic of her, cause she hardly speaks to anyone, unless, I guess, if she takes special liking to the person. It is most extra-ordinary – not to mention that she is the most extraordinary woman I have ever met. It must have been an attitude she acquired during the war. Before she went away she informed me that a fine young man would come to collect her prescriptions for her. She already told me your name; unconditional trust, that's what she has for you."

"She'd said that to me at one time," says Morris, "How is her health?"

"Nothing unusual for someone her age, - aches and pains and of course high blood pressure. This is how much I know, she refuses to go for a check-up. On the whole, she can be stubborn at times and she has a sound mind."

They shake hands and Morris leaves the consulting room and goes back into the reception area to say goodbye.

Receptionist asks Morris if she could have his phone number?

Morris writes his phone number on a piece of paper and gives it to her.

Lady patient says to the Receptionist, "shouldn't you have asked if he was married before asking for his number."

"I don't mind whether he is married or not. I want a piece of that brilliant mind and sexy body. Wouldn't you? Asks Receptionist.

"Too late for that now, I could be his grandmother". Replies Lady Patient.

Morris smiles and walks to the front door.

"Hope to see you again soon. You are a bit of fresh air. Says Lady Patient.

Morris leaves.

He goes to the chemist with the prescription and collects the medicines. On his way home he visits WH Smith's and purchases a large padded envelope before heading back to his house. As he packages the medicines into the large envelope, Morris finds the piece of paper which contains the address in Israel where the elderly lady would be staying; he surprisingly notices that she did not include her name but only the address. He is now faced with a puzzle, as she did not tell him what her name was, and he did not ask.

However, Morris decides to use the name on the back of the envelope that he picked up from her house. He addresses the envelope and goes down to the post office, which is only a short walk away.

On his way home, Morris is satisfied that one important task has been accomplished. He takes out his phone and notices there is a missed call. He quickly retrieves the number of the caller. It is his friend, Anthony, and he is right as he had guessed. Anthony, who inherited a fortune, is free and single with no responsibility and had been an alcohol abuser. He makes a genuine effort to refrain from abusing alcohol, with the help of Morris, but occasionally slips back into it when he is bored. Several thoughts were conflicting in Morris's mind. Anthony always leaves a message whenever he fails to speak to him. On occasions, when he did not, he had been helplessly drunk and would stay in, sleeping for days on end without food. He would leave his front door open throughout the whole period that he was incapacitated.

As Morris is struggling with the thought in his mind, he recalls a time when he was in the United States as a young man in his teens. He met a beautiful girl on a subway and they planned to go out on the town that evening. Morris went to pick the girl up from the address of the apartment block in Queens, which the girl gave him. When he pulled up at the address, clutching a bunch of flowers, he went to the front door which was not shut but ajar. He knocked but there was no answer. He stood there for a while checking that the door was the correct address, and it was. He slowly stepped in and proceeded through the entrance hall calling the girl's name and expecting an answer but to no avail.

He opened the lounge door slowly and peeped in to find the girl lying unconsciously on a settee with a needle stuck in her arm. He was motionless with fright and confusion. Looking at the small table by the side of the settee, he noticed that it was adorned with drug fixation apparatus. At that moment, he understood the scene unfolding before him. Should he have stayed and helped or should he simply have left the apartment believing that what he had witnessed was not real? If he'd taken the former, it may have meant that the girl may have simply died. If he'd taken the later, the girl may have survived and he and she might have been in trouble with the police, even though Morris was not an accomplice. How was he going to convince the police that he had no hand whatsoever in that stupid and catastrophic incident? He had to do something and quickly.

He picked up the phone, dialled the emergency unit and made a very rapid exit.

In this way, the emergency unit would have arrived, the girl may have been saved and he would have been free of implication. He noted that inevitably it was a win-win situation.

With this recollection, Morris rushes into his house, picks up the car keys and rushes out to his car and tries to start it, but it won't start. He tries again and again and finally the engine revs into life. His car has been methodically developing awkward signs of fatigue; this has been occurring intermittently lately, especially whenever he is in a great hurry to get to somewhere.

He quickly drives to Anthony's house and is pleasantly surprised. Anthony's car is not there, which means that he is not at home, and the front door is locked. Everything seems to be in order, so Morris exhales with a deep sense of relief. He sits in his car in front of Anthony's house looking around the surroundings, and recalls past incidents.

Anthony lives in a large Georgian house overlooking the golf course. The golf course is surrounded by woodland. The trees, with their large intertwining branches and leaves, provide perfect shade for the land beneath them. In summer, Anthony and his old public school mates would ride horses into these woods and stop to have a picnic. On summer's nights, the moonlight illuminating through these branches establishes sporadic light spots; the sound of birds providing rhythmic melodies creates an environment of a wonderful work of art that is totally magical.

On one summer's night, on Anthony's twenty-first birthday, Anthony decided to have a party; about fifty names were on his invitation list. However, he had never hosted a party before and therefore had no clue of what to provide, quantity-wise, or where to get them from. He spent most of his life in a boarding school and only came home on holidays. Nevertheless, he was determined to have a party. So, he equipped himself with a telephone directory and erratically started ordering everything he wanted for the party. This caused a traffic jam around his neighbourhood, with scores of delivery vans and Lorries taking various kinds of cooked food, drinks, cigarettes, fruits, chocolates and anything else he could think of to his house. He was full of self-praise that he had managed to organise the party alone and had got everything he needed, without assistance from anyone; he proudly wanted it that way.

In the late evening, when some of his guests started turning up, and were about to help themselves to the sumptuous array of food, which had been laid out by those who delivered it, Anthony disappointingly realised that there was an insufficient number of plates, knives and forks. At this point, it was too late to order some and have them delivered.

He had been trying not to let Morris know of this arrangement because he wanted to carry it out alone without any advice from anyone. It seemed to have backfired; he had to inform Morris, since it was the only way he could get a full supply of sufficient stock he so desperately needed. He called Morris and informed him of his predicament.

When Morris got to Anthony's house with cartons full of plates, knives and forks, he was dumbfounded with the amount of consumables that had been bought by Anthony for the party.

However, the following morning after the party, the swimming pool was littered with bottles of vodka, brandy, champagne, cans of beer, cigarette packets, plates with half eaten food still on them, and even some ladies' bras and knickers could be seen floating on the surface. It was not apparent there was water underneath, just a pile of rubbish. The memories of the party came flooding back in Morris's mind.

As Morris is in deep contemplation, Anthony pulls up in his classic X-Type Jaguar car, and is pleasantly surprised to see him, as usual.

"What's up Morris?" Asks Anthony

"I got a missed call and you did not leave a message, obviously I wrongly assumed you were on a bender again." Replies Morris.

Anthony defensively says, "Not at all, I don't touch the stuff anymore" he pauses, "well, only sometimes."

"Good! So what's happened?" Asks Morris.

"Some girls came round and I have just dropped them off at the train station."

Morris asks, "Is Henrietta one of them?"

"No, I wish she was. Not heard from that girl. Did you call her?" Asks Anthony.

"No." Replies Morris.

Morris gets out of his car and they go into Anthony's house for a chat and coffee. Anthony can be quite good at getting the girls but none of them has succeeded in staying with him for more than one or two meetings. This is mind-boggling because he is a good-natured young man who has everything that is but a dream to most young men. It is likely that his shortcomings could be attributed to his isolated upbringing. However, he is fortunate to have met Morris who has taken up the challenge to put him on the straight and narrow.

"I do fancy theatre tonight." Says Morris.

"Who are you going with?" Asks Anthony.

"Miah" Replies Morris.

Miah is an Anglo-Korean girl who graduated in Arts. She was looking for accommodation near to her college and Morris took her in as a tenant for six months. She left after her graduation but has remained in touch with him ever since. They meet up quite regularly.

"I quite like Miah, she is beautiful and well-rounded." Says Anthony.

"That's fine, but you have not experienced her eruptive anger. You will not like her when you see her angry", says Morris.

Chapter 5

When Morris gets home that evening, he calls Henrietta. She picks up the phone. She is not expecting his call because she did not give him her number and he did not ask. It has also been a long while since they parted.

"Hello", Answers Henrietta.

"How are you?" asks Morris:

"Who is this?" Enquires Henrietta

"It's me, Morris, remember? I gave you a lift from the airport."

Henrietta is shocked as she does not expect to hear from Morris and the phone drops from her hand. Morris is aware of what is happening so holds on to his phone waiting for her to come back. Henrietta stands staring at her phone that is lying on the floor. It is the most extraordinary concoction of astonishment, fright and delight. She reaches for her phone tentatively. And she asks:

"Are you there?"

"Yes, what is the matter? I told you I would call you" says Morris

"You did, but how …how did you get my number?" Asks Henrietta

"Never mind that, are you free this evening?" Asks Morris.

Henrietta does not hesitate and says, "Yes!"

"Okay, I will meet you at Starbuck's, opposite the station at 8pm." Says Morris.

"I will be there". Says Henrietta.

It is mixed feelings for her. On one hand, she is immensely pleased that she is going to meet up with that wonderful guy again, but on the other hand, she can't understand his deep and most profound nature. She keeps wondering how he got her phone number. That is the tapestry she would like to unfold when they meet again.

By 7.30pm Henrietta is already in Starbuck's directing her gaze at anybody that comes in through the door, in expectation that it could be Morris.

At exactly 8pm. he majestically appears by the door and Henrietta beckons at him to come over to her table. Morris notices her and proceeds to her table where Henrietta joyfully gives him a very firm embrace.

"Very nice to see you again Morris." Henrietta says delightfully.

"I'm glad too. You look so well, have you settled in your new flat?" asks Morris

"I found another flat, but it is only for six months so I will be looking again for another one". Replies Henrietta.

"Why, don't you like this one?" asks Morris.

"The landlord only gives six monthly contracts". She replies.

"Don't worry about it, you will find a good flat." Says Morris.

"Why are you confident about that?" Asks Henrietta.

"You'll find a better flat. By the way, do you fancy theatre tonight?" Morris asks.

"Yes, I love the theatre."

"Great, let's go."

As they get into Morris's car, he proceeds directly to his house. Henrietta is not perturbed in the least.

Morris in a calm voice says, "this is my house, should you be wondering why we are here instead of the theatre, it is because a friend of mine will be joining us, she will be here in about thirty minutes."

"I couldn't care less as long as I am with you." says Henrietta.

Morris's house comprises of a large lounge, kitchen and bathroom downstairs and three large bedrooms upstairs. The garden is quite large and alive with various flowers. The interior is moderately furnished and clean. He shows Henrietta round the house.

"Do you live here just by yourself?" Henrietta asks.

"Yes, I have done for five years." Replies Morris.

Have you ever thought of getting married?

"I was married. I also have two children.

"Do you see them?"

"Quite often."

"Where is your ex-wife now?"

"They are all here, in the UK."

Henrietta's thoughts are by now in conflict with why a woman would leave a guy like Morris, or is there another dark side to him that he keeps muted.

Chapter 6

The doorbell rings and Morris goes to the door. As he opens it, Miah enters. She is wearing a silk-like hugging dress that silhouettes her thin body, showing off her tantalizingly feminine features.

Morris introduces Miah to Henrietta and vice versa, and goes into his bedroom to get changed, leaving the two ladies in the lounge.

The silence that ensues between the two ladies can be cut with a knife. They seem to be thinking the same thing; each wondering if the other is Morris's girlfriend.

"How long have you known him?" enquires Miah.

"About two weeks" says Henrietta, "and you?"

"I have known Morris for a long time – a few years maybe. I lived here when I was at the art college; he is very considerate. I had to move nearer to the college for my studies so I put an ad in a local paper and received a call to view the spare room upstairs. At first, I was not quite sure whether to accept the offer or not; living with a man you hardly know can be a dangerous gamble. It turned out fine in the end and I am very pleased that I did take it. I learnt a lot from him and he's always got time for everyone, without prejudice.

"How re-assuring." Say Henrietta.

"I left this house long ago, but we still remain very good friends"

"So he is your boyfriend." Asks Henrietta.

Not quite like that. Although I have made several passes at him to understand that I really, really fancy him, but he remains indifferent. He treats me like a princess, very nice indeed, better than one's boyfriend would treat one. One night, I got so frustrated and angry that I kicked at his television and broke it I also kicked his bathroom door down.

"Why did you do that?" Asks Henrietta.

"Like I said, I got frustrated. I had given him several signs that I really love him and wanted to be his girlfriend, but he was still indifferent, so I went mad. He always says that I have an eruptive anger but he is always cool amid turmoil, chaos and harsh realities of life. I mean, he is spiritually very strong. Don't misunderstand me...we have got it together at times and I can tell you he is quite a man, but he is not the one to take advantage of anyone. No man has ever loved me like that before. He is strong and tender at the same time and knows all the spots and how and when to work them. As a result, you won't want the ecstasy to stop."

Just at that point, Morris re-enters from the bedroom and heads for the front door. The two ladies get up and follow him. They are off to the theatre.

Very late at night, they leave the theatre and proceed to the village restaurant in Wimbledon. After indulging in a sumptuous dinner, they start making their way to the car:

Morris asks, "Which one of you do I have to drop off first?"

"I haven't got the key to my flat; it seems I have to go home in the morning." Replies Henrietta.

"You may drop me off then". Requests Miah.

Morris drops Miah off and takes Henrietta back to his house. He goes straight to the wine cupboard in the lounge and pours two glasses of wine, one for himself and the other for Henrietta.

"I would like a shower". Says Henrietta.

"That's Okay," says Morris.

Morris enters his bedroom and re-enters the lounge clutching a dressing gown and a towel. Henrietta slowly steps forward to reach Morris and embraces him very warmly as if her life depended on it. They start to kiss and groan, and as the kissing goes on for a long while, Henrietta begins to undo the zip of Morris's jeans. He detaches himself from her and gently leads her to the bathroom, gives her a peck on the cheek, shuts the bathroom door behind him and leaves her to take a shower. He quickly goes into the spare room and changes the sheets. He returns to the lounge and begins to sip the glass of wine. After a short while, she enters the lounge with a towel tied round her upper body revealing truly nice pair of legs.

Henrietta walks straight to Morris and sits on his lap. He reaches for the other glass of wine and passes it to her. There is silence as they cuddle each other, and occasionally sip the wine. By this time, it is gone two in the morning. Morris suddenly extracts himself from Henrietta's intense cuddle, holds her hand, and gently pulls her up from the sofa and leads her to the spare room. Henrietta is aware that she is going to sleep in the spare room alone.

"Is this where I am going to sleep?" Asks Henrietta.

"Yes, you will be comfortable". Says Morris.

"Where are you going to sleep?" Asks Henrietta.

"Next door, in my bedroom."

Henrietta looks disappointed but gives him a kiss anyway. He says good night to her and goes to his bedroom, lifts the bed covers and slides into bed.

About an hour and a half later—as he is falling asleep – he hears his bedroom door creek slowly. He takes no notice as he always leaves the door slightly ajar for circulation of air, and then there's another gentle creek; this time a naked figure tip-toes through the doorway and stands right by the side of Morris's bed. As he looks up in the darkness, it is certainly Henrietta.

"Come into bed before you catch a cold". Says Morris.

Morris lifts the bed covers up for Henrietta and she slides into bed with him. In the morning, Morris gets up, has a shower. Henrietta is still in a deep sleep. He leaves her a note.

If you wake up before I get back, do help yourself to breakfast. I hope you will find something you like.

Chapter 7

It has been a few days since Morris last visited the elderly lady's house, so he decides to go in case there are letters that may need his attention. Morris leaves his house and shuts the front door gently as not to wake Henrietta and proceeds to number fifty-one; the elderly lady's house.

He walks into the house and finds three letters with *Dr. A. Bozivich* as the addressee. Two of the letters seem to be private and one has a Russian embassy stamp printed on the back of the envelope. He leaves the letters on the carpet next to the wall behind the front door and decides to go upstairs as he only saw downstairs the first time he visited. He ascends the stairs, clearing the cobwebs that obstruct his way. There are two large bedrooms each decorated with expensive antique furnishings and the floor is laced with thick rugs. From the state of the rooms and the whole surroundings, it is apparent that no one has been up there in years - all cobwebs and mouldy smells. He very swiftly finds his way downstairs, shuts the front door behind him and hurries back to his house.

He gets in to find Henrietta sitting in the lounge watching television with a cup of tea in her hand.

"What can I get you?" Asks Henrietta.

"It's okay, I will help myself." Morris replies "Are you fine with the breakfast?"

"Absolutely fine, thank you." Says Henrietta.

"You seem to be making yourself at home". Says Morris.

"I haven't felt at home like this for a very long time". Henrietta confirms.

"Excellent!" Says Morris, "I am happy that you are happy."

Morris enters the kitchen and fries up some eggs and puts them on top of a couple of pieces of toast, which he ate in no time at all. He comes back into the lounge.

"Excuse me, do you mind if I turn the television off for a while?" Morris asks, "It's time for my ceremony in the air. You may join me or you can watch if you like".

Henrietta repeats questioningly, "Ceremony in the air?" "No, I do not mind – please switch it off."

Henrietta is excited as she wants to see what Morris is about to do, so she flicks the remote button and the television is switched off.

Morris moves to the far side of the lounge; his meditation area. In this area, there is a table, on this table there is a small casing like a box, inside the box is a scroll. In front of the box are two candles in a couple of candle stands and a small silver container which he filled with water. On the floor in front of the table is a bell. He takes out a string of beads from a pouch and starts to recite and chant.

Henrietta is filled with admiration as she watches and listens as Morris hits the bell and focuses on the scroll while reciting and chanting. Differing thoughts keep wandering through her mind. Could this be the reason why he has such unselfish, positive and rounded characteristic, and always happy? She is thinking that if that was the reason, she would want some of it, if only he would teach her. Now she has more questions to ask him but needs to find the right time. The sound of the powerful rhythm is increasingly harmonious and soothing that she falls comfortably asleep.

Thirty minutes later, Morris completes the practice. He gets up from the chair and turns round to find Henrietta sleeping like a baby on the sofa. Morris takes a book from the shelf and starts reading silently. After a while, Henrietta wakes up refreshed.

"I have to go now," says Henrietta.

"Why?" Morris asks.

"I need to go to the library to look up the census register".

"Are you looking for someone?"

"Yes. I will tell you about it later".

Morris grabs his car keys and they leave the house. It is Saturday morning, and as they drive passed a supermarket, Morris decides to pull in to the car park.

Morris says to Henrietta, "I need to pop in here to get a couple of things, won't be long".

"Okay," replies Henrietta.

Morris proceeds to the supermarket. At the entrance is a beggar; he is unshaven and in his late teens and asks Morris for some money for breakfast. Morris glances at him and makes his way to the flower section and purchases a nice bunch of roses and makes his way back to the exit. The beggar asks him again for some money. Morris stops and engages with the beggar in conversation.

"What is your name?" Asks Morris:

"Isabbul." Replies the beggar.

"So you are hungry?" Asks Morris.

"I have not eaten real food for three days". Replies Isabbul.

Morris points at the empty cans of beer and a half-empty can beside Isabbul on the floor.

Morris says, "Drinking all these early in the morning is not good for your health when you have not eaten for three days".

Isabbul feels guilty that Morris has discovered his indulgence.

"I won't judge your actions, but if you want something to eat - come with me," says Morris.

Isabbul hurriedly puts the empty beer cans in a plastic bag and follows Morris. As they approach the car, Henrietta notices that Morris is clutching a bunch of roses but is wondering why a man so emaciated and in such a rough and dirty condition is following him. On the other hand, it was not such a surprise to her, for as far as Morris is concerned, he embraces everyone irrespective of their circumstances. However, she is very keen to know what the story would be.

When they reach the car, Morris opens the front door and hands over the roses to Henrietta and kisses her on the lips. He then introduces Isabbul to her. He opens the back door for Issabul and they drive off. Henrietta hopes for some detailed introduction about who Issabul really is because Morris only introduced them by their names. She expects a detailed introduction but is not forthcoming and she asks.

"What is the connection between you and Isabbul - Morris?"

Morris replies, "He is hungry and I am hungry so we will have some breakfast together".

"I thought you just had breakfast." Says Henrietta.

"Yes, but I just happen to be hungry again". Replies Morris.

Isabbul cuts in, "Madam, I asked your husband for some money to have something to eat and he asked if I was hungry and I said yes and he asked me to follow him".

"Typical!" Exclaims Henrietta.

"Isabbul, thank you for thinking this pretty lady was my wife but do not be disappointed that we are not married". Says Morris.

"That's a pity because you both complement each other in persona and maybe in character, I guess". Says Isabbul.

"Very kind, thank you, but what would you like for breakfast?"

"McDonalds, sir", says Isabbul, "I could murder a BigMac."

"McDonalds it is then", Isabbul, Morris assures, "and please call me Morris, not 'sir'.

"Okay sir". Says Isabbul.

"Please ignore the word "sir," says Morris.

"I'll remember, sir." Says Isabbul.

"Oh no, I mean, replace the word 'sir' with 'Morris', that is my name". Morris says with frustration.

"I'll remember, Morris". Replies Isabbul.

Morris is pleased and says, "correct".

Morris turns to Henrietta.

"When will you be back from the census office?"

"Don't know, but it may not be later than 4pm with a bit of luck".

Morris retract his phone number on his phone and passes his phone to Henrietta.

"Call me on this number when you get back".

Henrietta enters the number on her phone.

"Thanks, I will call you," says Henrietta.

"Where shall I drop you off," asks Morris, "I don't even know where you live".

"Could you stop opposite the train station"?

Morris pulls up opposite the station and Henrietta kisses him on the cheek and gets out the car and Morris drives off with Isabbul.

"Can I come in the front seat?" asks Isabbul.

"It's not necessary. Relax in the back; be chauffeur-driven today."

Morris turns round at the roundabout and heads to the car park behind the station and parks his car. He takes Isabbul to the McDonalds situated on the top floor of a shopping centre and asks him to order whatever he wants to eat. Isabbul orders a BigMac and fries and a large cappuccino. Morris orders small fries and a small Americano. He has had breakfast and just wants to keep Isabbul company. Most of all he rather prefers that Isabbul has some food instead of giving him some money with which to purchase cans of strong beer. While they sit down consuming what they ordered, Morris notices that Isabbul is gulping his BigMac very fast, displaying a sign of one who is starving. Within a few minutes, he has finished his meal and drank the whole cappuccino. Morris has not even started on his fries, so he pushes them across to Isabbul, who grabs them and scoffs all of them in no time at all. Morris is watching him with compassion and satisfaction.

"Tell me about yourself," Morris asks.

"Not a lot to tell really," says Isabbul.

"Do you live somewhere?" Asks Morris.

"I live at the most famous address in London". Replies Isabbul.

"Buckingham Palace?" Asks Morris.

"No. Under f*****g Waterloo Bridge". Replies Isabbul.

"I beg your pardon! Mind your language". Says Morris.

"I am sorry Morris". Isabbul apologises.

"How do you sustain yourself, such as food and things?" Asks Morris

"Sometimes I busk at tube stations, sometimes, I steal food from supermarkets and sometimes I beg for food. I get by". Says Isabbul:

"What instrument do you busk with?"

"F********g guitar. The only thing I have always wanted to do is play the guitar, and I am bloody good".

"Where is your guitar?" Morris asks.

"Nicked by some idiot who cannot even play the guitar. He may flog it for a few quid for some beers, it's a shame." Says Isabbul.

"Where do you come from originally?" Asks Morris.

"Turkey. I was adopted by English couple when I was eight and I am eighteen now. They are good couple, they bought me the guitar on my sixteenth birthday and I have been playing it ever since, until it got nicked by some idiot who used to live under the Waterloo Bridge with me. I heard he is now in Scotland, so there is no chance of getting it back". Replies Isabbul.

"Where are your adopted parents?" Asks Morris.

"They used to live in Poole, Dorset, but I have not seen them since my sixteenth birthday. Perhaps, they have died or left the place because last time I phoned, the number did not exist and I sent a card when I stayed in a hostel but got no reply". Replies Isabbul.

"Why did you come to London?"

"When I was in Poole I used to go to see my friend who played the guitar like Jimmy Hendricks and stayed with him all day and night playing the guitar. When I got home early in the mornings, I was locked out. It happened all the time. So, one day, just a few days after my birthday in April, I carried my rucksack and left for London and have not been home since. They were quite elderly, so, may be they have gone to heaven. (Pause) May I ask you something?" asks Isabbul.

"Anything you like." Says Morris.

"Where are you from originally, Africa?" Asks Isabbul.

"That's right. I am from West Africa". Morris acknowledges.

"And why are you kind to me?" Asks Isabbul.

"Everyone needs a little help sometimes, and I mean everyone." Says Morris.

"Millionaires don't need help". Says Isabbul.

"Wrong." Morris says.

"Tell me, what are the most important attributes in life?" Asks Isabbul

"Wisdom, courage, compassion and life force". Replies Morris.

There is silence. Isabbul is deep in thought trying to make sense of the four words. Morris is relaxed, enthusiastically waiting for further questions. Isabbul collects himself and stares at Morris with some sort of curiosity.

"So not wealth then? I mean, loads of money – like winning the jackpot on a lottery." Says Isabbul.

Morris, emphatically says, "No!" Morris continues, "Money is great, but not as important as one's true virtues. It is what one chooses to do with money that matters. If it is for your benefit and for the benefit of others, then it is constructively important and one is worthy and noble and will result in a good cause and good effect. Other than that, it can be negative and destructive. It is pitiful that in this day and age some people tend to measure happiness with the amount of money one has accumulated. One who genuinely strives for one's happiness and the happiness of others is the true victor in life and the only path to absolute freedom".

"That's really cool. You make a lot of sense and you say powerful things. I have never spent some quality time which is as enlightening as this before". Says Isabbul.

Isabbul stands up to go and shakes Morris's hand. "Thank you very much, I have got to go now and hope I have not taken up all your time."

"Like money, time does not really matter; it is what one does with time that matters". Says Morris.

"Cool! You're a legend." Exclaims Isabbul.

Morris unleashes an explosive kind of laughter that turns heads from all around. His characteristic laughter portends great joy and hope, uninhibited and unarguably stress-free. His infectious laughter triggers a multitude of smiles and laughter; Isabbul falls into an uncontrollable fit of laughter as a result. They leisurely make their way out of McDonalds.

"Did you say your birthday was in April?" Asks Morris.

"April first to be exact." Replies Isabbul.

"That's in a couple of weeks". Says Morris.

"Do you usually shop in that supermarket?" Asks Isabbul.

"I occasionally pop in, for small stuff". Replies Morris.

"Such as flowers?" asks Isabbul.

"Not necessarily". Says Morris.

As they reach the front of the shopping centre, Isabbul thanks Morris and about to depart -

"So, I take it you do not require a lift". Says Morris.

Isabbul, feeling his stomach says, "No, I am full now and I am done for today."

"Just be careful under that famous address," says Morris, "I will see you again."

Isabbul is taken aback by Morris's apparent confidence.

"What makes you so sure you'll see me again?" Asks Isabbul.

"We will meet again". Confidently says Morris.

Morris goes to the car park, gets in his car and drives home.

Chapter 8

It is at noon of that Saturday, that he accidentally finds the business card given to him by Mr Knight, who offered to purchase his old Mercedes car. Morris decides to give him a call.

Mr Knight is ecstatic on receiving Morris's call and promises Morris he would come over to his house to take the car. He asks for his address, which Morris gives to him. Forty minutes, later Mr Knight arrives with his son and examines the car thoroughly in front of Morris's house, while Morris stands by his front door, watching. After a few minutes, Mr Knight approaches Morris, takes out his wallet and counts the sum of money, which is triple what the car is worth, and gives it to Morris. Morris counts the money and writes out a receipt.

"Are you getting another car?" Asks Mr Knight.

"Yes, I have to. I always need a car," replies Morris.

"Come to my garage, I may have a car that is just right for you", says Mr Knight.

Morris locks his front door and gets in Mr Knight's car while Mr Knight's son drives Morris's car back to their garage.

In the garage there are many cars, so Morris is walking from one car to the order in an effort to choose a car.

Mr Knight enters his office, collects a bunch of car keys and gives them to his son and instructs him to show Morris a particular car. Morris follows his son to a very nice spotless silver-coloured car with cream leather interior, sun roof, air conditioning and walnut dash. Morris immediately falls in love with it and takes it for a test drive. He discovers that the car is smooth and the engine is quiet and drives like a dream. All the gadgets are in good working order. He returns to the garage:

"How much are you selling this car for?" Asks Morris.

"Are you happy with it?" Asks Mr Knight.

I have to take it, it's a very nice car'. Replies Morris.

"I can see you are a good-natured young man so I will give you a good deal". Says Mr Knight.

In the end, Mr Knight accepts an amount far less than he paid Morris for his old car. The new car is bigger, both in size and engine capacity. They exchange paper-work and Morris telephones his insurers and gets a new policy. They shake hands. Mr Knight's son tells Morris that the car was brought in by an ex-ambassador with a private number plate and part-exchanged it for a smaller car. What's more, it has just got a new MOT and a long road fund licence, and was serviced twice a year. Morris is pleased and gratified. He enters his new car and drives away.

He is just about one minute to his house when his phone rings. It is Henrietta. She tells him that she is just about to leave the census office. Morris asks if her mission went well at the census office and she replies that she got more confused with the entries in the register. Morris tells her not to worry and asks her if she is free the following day, which is Sunday.

"Yes," she replies.

"I will pick you up from Starbuck's in the afternoon for lunch," says Morris.

When he arrives at his house, Morris goes straight to his meditation area and spends twenty minutes meditating and reading some books and magazines that relate to his practice of philosophy. Later in the same evening, he cracks some eggs and makes a simple omelette and vegetables and stays in all night. As his neighbours pass by, they stopped to admire his new car which is parked in front of his house, and guess if it belongs to him or perhaps to his visitor. Since his old Mercedes is not in sight, some of them assume that it might belong to his guest or his friend.

In the afternoon of the following day, he drives to Starbucks to meet Henrietta. She is already seated in a corner with a cup of coffee and periodically glances at the front door expecting Morris to come in at any moment.

As soon as he comes in through the door, she stands up making her way towards the door to meet him. So, they immediately leave Starbucks. Henrietta is excited to meet Morris again, not only because she was very happy in his company the previous night but also because she has a lot of questions to ask him. She is expecting to find Morris's old Mercedes, but to her surprise he leads her to a new and luxurious car. Her jaws drop and she freezes on the spot as he opens the door and holds it for her to enter. She is speechless as she approaches the car with apparent caution and bewilderment. She gets in and Morris goes to the driver's door and gets in, starts the car and drives off. There is silence and she is looking round the front and back interior, admiring every aspect of the new XG 30.

"How many cars have you got?" asks Henrietta.

"Just this one". Replies Morris.

"So, the other one did not belong to you?" Asks Henrietta.

"It was mine but I got this one yesterday". Replies Morris.

"You never seize to amaze, or you could be a silent millionaire". Says Henrietta.

"It's none of that nonsense". Says Morris.

"Do you call that nonsense; one minute you are driving an old car and the next you drive an almost brand new car, epitomising ultimate luxury and comfort and you call it nonsense". Says Henrietta.

"When one is of the sun, the universe provides and protects one. Just think of what you really need and it will come without fail. It is not really all about money or being a millionaire. To have plenty of money is fine if one uses it for his happiness and others happiness too, but when one is of the sun, one has everything one needs and one uses it for the benefit of all, not just for one's self". Says Morris.

"What do you mean by 'of the sun'" Asks Henrietta.

"When you really, really seek, then you will find and when you find you will make the sound of the sun and it's only then that you will definitely understand". Explains Morris.

"And then what?" Asks Henrietta.

"You will be completely free". Replies Morris.

"Free from what?" Asks Henrietta.

"As I said, you will definitely understand - that is the way of the sun". Replies Morris.

Morris pulls up in front of a restaurant in Wimbledon Village, where there are numerous other restaurants, and asks her to pick out one to have lunch in. She looks around and goes for "Café Rouge". They go in and have lunch.

On their way out of the restaurant, Henrietta asks, "Where are we off to next?"

To which Morris replies, "Be patient, it's just around the corner."

They get in the car and Morris drives off heading further down the road towards the common. He parks the car by the common and holds Henrietta's hand as they stroll into the woods opposite Anthony's house. The sun, which is unhindered by the bright clouds, illuminates the ground in the woods in crimson and gold sporadic spots through the broad leaves of the trees; the sound of birds provide a philharmonic background sound; the woods are tranquil and almost empty except for the occasional passing of couples on horseback, adventuring and picnicking at the far side of the woods.

Morris picks a spot near the pond and sits on an exposed root of a very large tree. Henrietta is so delirious and excited about this magical environment that she keeps wandering around with excitement. Morris is silent but casually throws some stones in the pond intermittently.

After a while, Henrietta returns to Morris and sits next to him resting her head on his shoulder. Morris glances at her, she raises her head and he notices her eyes exuding complete submission and contentment. They smile and she leans closer still to him.

"How do you feel?" Asks Morris.

"Totally fulfilled." Replies Henrietta.

"What brought you to the UK?" Asks Morris.

"In search of my nan. I last saw her when I was five, that was thirty years ago and as I recollect the meeting was brief and rather disastrous". Replies Henrietta.

"Where was that?" Asks Morris.

"In Australia". Replies Henrietta, "She came on holiday and my mother heard from some-one that she was in Australia. One morning, my mother took me to the beach; there I was playing with my friend who was about the same age as myself – you know, we were running around in the sand and suddenly, as I looked back, my mother was seriously arguing with an old woman who was wearing a bikini and smoking a long cigarette. So, I ran to my mother and held her legs so tight. The elderly woman looked at me very compassionately and lovingly. She tried to lift me up in her arms but I resisted as I did not know who she was and she was arguing loudly with my mother, creating an ugly scene at the beach. My mother also shouted at her not to touch me. Suddenly, the woman moved away to her deck chair, picked up her things and left the beach. By this time, some crowd had gathered, wondering what was happening. My little friend's mother asked my mother who the elderly woman was and my mother explained that she was my nan".

"Did your mother know she was at the beach?" asks Morris.

"It was totally by accident, though someone had told her she was in Australia, on holiday". Says Henrietta.

"What urged you to start looking for her?" Asks Morris.

"Her disconnection from my mother has created a very bad rift in the family, to the point that I don't know any other members of the family except my mother. I am sure I have uncles and aunties, perhaps even nieces and nephews, but it is only my mother that I have seen and know of. I have no idea about my family history and my mother does not say anything about them, so, I guess it is for me to find out. I have searched for her in Poland, Germany and Russia to no avail; I am now searching for her here in the UK". Replies Henrietta.

"What is your father's stand on all this?" Asks Morris.

"My father divorced my mother a very long time ago and she remarried and divorced again. To my understanding, none of the two men she had married knew anything about her family". Says Henrietta.

"So, what made you think your nan could be here?" Asks Morris.

"Because, I overheard my mother speaking to some-one on the telephone, she said to the person that my nan may never leave the UK like she left other countries because she is quite elderly now. So, I really hope that she is here". Replies Henrietta.

"Why did you look for her in Poland, Russia and Germany?" Asks Morris.

"Before I overheard my mother on the telephone, I had already been to those countries to search for her as they were the most likely places she could live". Replies Henrietta.

Morris, who has been listening attentively, rises from the root where they are sitting, leaving Henrietta still sitting on the root. He starts to walk about in silent wonder as she focuses her gaze at him. After a short while, he approaches her, takes her hand and pulls her up from the root and gives her a firm embrace and holds it for a while.

"I will do whatever I can to help you. My promise is that if your nan is here in the UK we will find her",

"Thank you Morris, I have never felt so secure like this in my whole life – you are the most extraordinary human being, in every way". Says Henrietta

"That is the virtue of a human being" – there is nothing extraordinary about it. Everyone has the potential to become really human. All one has to do is to polish one's life in order to return to being a true human being. True human beings detest gang warfare or any type of warfare; after all, there is no misunderstanding or dispute that cannot be resolved through genuine mutual respect, patience and continuous dialogue, not by selfishness and desire to dominate. They strive to become happy and relieve others of suffering so that they become happy too. True happiness is really not the exclusion of problems or hardship but the confidence and the ability to solve the problem or hardship. It means that one is happy irrespective of one's circumstances. That is absolute happiness. It is not the kind of relative or transient happiness that most people tend to seek, such as wealth and power in the knowledge that everything is in constant flux. What happens if one is rich and powerful today and tomorrow one is not – it is not rocket science to understand that it will cause that person suffering and shame. Some go as far as being suicidal; can you now see how necessary it is to acquire absolute happiness instead of relative or transient happiness?" Asks Morris.

"That's an amazing philosophy", says Henrietta, "but how does one do that? I mean, how does one acquire such virtue?"

"In addition to what I have explained already, one needs to respect the life of all living beings", says Morris.

"That's controversial is it not – worms, snakes, flies, dogs and cats are living beings, how does one respect them?" Asks Henrietta.

Morris starts to explain, "Do not deny them life, do not hurt them – you must do your utmost best to respect their life because they share the same life's essence as us. To deny them of life is a bad cause and it brings suffering which is the effect of that cause. When one polishes one's life – joy, inner strength, compassion, wisdom and courage flow profusely and ceaselessly from one's life, and the whole of the universe will protect and provide for you as you take positive action to better yourself and others. It is really as simple as that".

"I can see clearly now how you got your new car". Says Henrietta.

"The car is simply like a side dish rather than the main meal". Replies Morris.

"When you polish your life, you will achieve the highest state of life and become purely human or in other words, enlightened. The difference between one who is truly enlightened and an ordinary person is that one who is enlightened has polished his life, while an ordinary person hasn't, therefore, is deluded. Everyone has the potential to become truly enlightened".

"What do you mean by "polishing one's life"? How do you polish your life? I have a bath daily and apply some very good cream afterwards, could that be termed as polishing my life?" Asks Henrietta.

At this point Morris erupts in his characteristic explosive and infectious laughter which causes Henrietta to laugh hysterically.

"I mean spiritually," says Morris, "for one to be able to gain absolute happiness and become enlightened one must first of all make the sound of the sun; with this sound, one's life will be correctly aligned three hundred and sixty degrees to the rhythm of the universe. When this happens, all negative tendencies or desires will be transformed to create value, and your positive aspects will emerge naturally and will be strengthened even further."

"Will you teach me how to make that sound?" Asks Henrietta.

"I will, I promise". Says Morris.

"Yes, I need some of that". Says Henrietta.

"Everybody does, but it is simply that they have no knowledge or have never heard of the sound; after all, everyone, without exception, yearns for true happiness". Says Morris.

"There are many questions I reserved to ask you today, but you have already answered most of them without me asking. I have no further questions. Your life is so different, it exudes hope, warmth and joy at all times.

My God! I want to be like that". Exclaims Henrietta.

Morris is in deep thought, focusing his gaze at nothing in particular. After a long silence, which is becoming interminable, he proceeds nearer to the pond which is close by and begins to throw stones in it while Henrietta silently watches.

"What are you thinking?" Asks Henrietta.

"You've been in the wars – you know, all the effort you have been making to find your nan and get your family together".

"Do you have any idea what it is like, not to have seen or know any member of my family except for my nan whom I only met once". Asks Henrietta.

"What's your nan's name?"

"I think her name is Maria"

"Did you say you think?" Asks Morris, "What did you search for in the census register?"

"Maria Kosokov". Replies Henrietta, "That's her maiden name; it is not what she could be called now. I understand that she was never married but fell in love with an Air Force officer during the war and changed her name."

With sudden realisation she looks at her watch.

"I need to go back to my flat to pack my bag and get my travelling papers ready." Says Henrietta.

"Travelling papers?" Asks Morris.

"Yes, I intend to go to Paris tomorrow morning. Replies Henrietta

"What for?" Asks Morris.

"My friend in Australia gave me an address of her auntie who lives in Paris. She will assist me in locating my nan if she was there". Says Henrietta.

Morris, unhesitant, holds Henrietta's hand as they leave the woods to walk back to the car. Morris stops and determinedly and directly looks into her eyes.

"We will find your nan, you have good intentions – noble intentions," says Morris.

Morris drops Henrietta off at her flat. On his way home, he cannot stop thinking what difficult circumstances she has been through. Then he wonders why her mother did not want to reveal anything to Henrietta about her family and could only resort to dismal information in order to find her nan, who she expects will disseminate details of what happened before or immediately after she was born. Perhaps, if she finds her nan, Henrietta might be able to find other members of her family and therefore, would be able to enjoy normal family life like other families. Morris concludes that whatever the case might be, Henrietta has very good intentions in endeavouring to reunite her family.

Early in the following morning, he receives a phone call from Henrietta.

"Hi Morris, just to let you know that I am now about to leave for Paris and will see you when I get back". Says Henrietta.

"What time is your flight?" Asks Morris.

"I will be going by train". Henrietta replies.

"Okay. Do you mind if I give you a lift to St Pancreas station?" Asks Morris.

"Oh! Will you?"

"Can I pick you up from Starbucks?"

"That will be great, Morris. Will 10am suit you?"

"Sure, see you at ten". Replies Morris.

When Morris pulls up at ten, Henrietta is already standing in front of Starbucks with a small suitcase. She walks up to the car and gets in. They drive off.

"Sure you got everything? Passport, ticket, toothbrush, hairbrush ... knickers...?" Asks Morris.

Henrietta gives him a cheeky smile.

"Yes, I have got everything that I need, including a pair of knickers," Henrietta replies.

"How did you buy the tickets?" Asks Morris.

"On the Internet". Replies Henrietta.

"Excellent. Did you have breakfast?" Asks Morris.

"Yes, thank you for being considerate. There is one question that I have been trying to ask you". Says Henrietta.

"Fire away". Says Morris.

"How did you get my phone number?" Asks Henrietta.

Morris delightfully says, "By the power of thought and power of belief. When you genuinely and strongly believe without any doubt, the universe will definitely turn those thoughts and beliefs and make them your reality. You must try and unleash the power of your life, persevering with strong conviction; it is the key to unlocking a brilliant future by bringing the sun of time-without-beginning to shine in your life – that is the way of the sun. It generates complete freedom," he continues.

"First and foremost, to really be able to do that, one has to make the sound of the sun. That puts your life in rhythm with life of the universe. It is only then you can taste the truth of that sound. As you practise making that sound, it enables you to draw on inexhaustible inner reserves of courage, hope and resilience to surmount challenges and expand your life, and to help others do the same. It is the most dynamic and compassionate life condition and you are truly happy irrespective of circumstances".

Henrietta who has been listening attentively, does not need any more proof from him, because she has seen the most extraordinary characteristics and behaviour from him that she is yearning to acquire such qualities as he possesses.

"Morris, I really, want to know about that sound and make it, but I have not got enough money to pay you to teach me how to make that sound". Says Henrietta.

"Oh no, it's your right, so you do not pay for it. It is free for everyone, it's everyone's entitlement to be happy; at peace and fulfil his or her life. So do not worry, I will teach you everything." Says Morris.

"So, you will teach me how to make that sound?" Asks Henrietta

"Definitely". Replies Morris.

Henrietta is thoughtful for a while.

"Do you know", Henrietta says, "I like reading books…all sorts of books and I have come across a book in which I read about a Buddha. In my recollection, what you have described is a depiction of a Buddha, any coloration with what you are talking about?"

"That's what I am talking about. Says Morris. "A Buddha is someone who has firmly established the life condition of Buddhahood as his or her most dominant state of life. Most people, however, are unaware of this possibility or how to actualise it. When a common mortal, that is, an ordinary person, becomes enlightened he or she becomes a Buddha. So, that means that we all have the potential to become Buddhas".

They are now approaching St. Pancreas International station. Morris veers into an entrance of a car park and is about to drive through the barrier when a young man approaches his car. He winds his window down, as he recognises the young man as Isabbul, the beggar whom he had taken to McDonalds for a breakfast the previous day. Isabbul is holding a bucket of water and a sponge. He does not recognise Morris.

"Hello Isabbul, what are you doing here?" Asks Morris.

Isabbul is startled by who he thinks is a complete stranger calling him by name. So he looks at Morris closely and recollects their peculiar meeting in a supermarket.

Isabbul with excitement says, "Forgive me sir, I did not recognise you in this flashy car, how many cars have you got?"

"Remember? Do not call me 'sir', you seem to have forgotten my name already". Says Morris.

"How can I forget, Morris". Says Isabbul.

"So what brought you here?" Asks Morris.

With some hesitation Isabbul replies, "I give the impression that I wash cars and collect money upfront".

"How much?" Morris asks, "You may wash my car someday".

"I won't do that to you, Morris. You see, when I collect money upfront, the person parks his car and leaves, hoping that his car would be washed by the time he or she returns, but I'll disappear with the money and the car is not washed. It is called 'self-preservation'. Just remember, if anyone asks to wash your car, and demands money upfront, do not fall for it." Warns Isabbul.

"That is stupid. Why don't you wash the cars and keep the money?" Asks Morris.

"I just don't." Says Isabbul.

Morris writes out his telephone number on a piece of paper and gives it to Isabbul.

"This is my phone number, give me a call. I am organising a birthday party for my friend on the first of April, so I am inviting you". Says Morris.

"Inviting me?" Asks Isabbul.

"Yes". Replies Morris.

"Quite a coincidence; it's my birthday too, the same date". Says Isabbul.

"Great, it will be nice to see you then". Says Morris.

"I will be there. I used to go to parties a long time ago. I like to party." says Isabbul.

"Be there." Affirms Morris.

"Last time, you said to me, 'We will meet again.' I did not believe you, and here we are". Says Isabbul.

"Life is full of surprises, Isabbul." Says Morris.

"It is like I have known you for ages". Says Isabbul.

Morris continues driving into the car park. As he is descending the ramp, he notices a man who looks like a tramp, in the corner. By the wall is a mattress and cardboard boxes improvised as his bed. He is aggressively beating up and kicking his dog. The dog is howling and struggling to escape but he is held on a lead which restricts him from escaping. To Morris's surprise, a few people are gathered, watching the scene, but none of them tries to stop the tramp. Some just enter their cars and drive off unconcerned.

Morris stops his car and angrily gets out, hurries and stands between the dog and the tramp in full view of the spectators.

He turns to the tramp and says calmly but firmly, "I don't care what this dog has done but you are not going to hit and kick him again."

The tramp is terrified of Morris. "This bloody animal has eaten my sausage roll", says the Tramp.

"But I won't let you hit or kick him again," Morris reiterates.

The tramp drops the lead and walks back to the mattress mumbling. The dog runs to a corner of the mattress and cowers. Morris gently approaches the dog and begins to stroke him.

He takes out his wallet and gives the tramp a ten pound note and says, "Get some sausage rolls for yourself and for your dog, but do not hit or kick him again."

The tramp looks at Morris, and then looks at the ten pound which he is holding in his hand, in disbelief. As Morris returns to his car, the spectators are fascinated and their heads turn; their eyes follow Morris until he gets in his car, where Henrietta is sitting and watching the whole episode. Morris drives his car in to a parking bay opposite where the incident took place and parks his car. The spectators are still transfixed, with dropped jaws, as Morris walks into St. Pancreas International station with Henrietta.

Fifty-five minutes later, Henrietta checks in and boards the train and is on her way to Paris.

Chapter 9

Morris returns to the car park to collect his car. To his amazement the car park is comparatively calm and tranquil. The tramp is sitting on his mattress eating some sausage rolls and drinking a can of strong beer, and the dog is settled down next to the tramp also munching a sausage roll. To Morris, it is a pretty sight.

He approaches the tramp and asks, "What is your name?"

The tramp raises his head, recognising Morris, "Kevin" he replies.

"Do you stay here all the time?" asks Morris

"This is me home, gimme a cigarette - guv". Says Kevin.

"I don't smoke, so I don't have a cigarette". Says Morris.

"You're alright - guv. Thanks for the money". Says Kevin

"That's alright. Take care of yourself". Says Morris.

Morris leaves, gets in his car and drives away.

On his way back to Wimbledon, traffic has formed and the road is littered with cars, which are sometimes stationary, and at times moving at snail's pace. His phone rings and he looks at the screen; it is Anthony trying to get hold of him but Morris chooses not to answer. He is waiting until he reaches a comfortable and safe spot to call him back as it is unlawful to use the telephone whilst driving. Suddenly, he discovers a side street, turns into it and pulls over. He calls Anthony, who answers immediately.

"Hi Morris, I have been trying to reach you", says Anthony, "where have you been?"

"I am in the traffic coming back from St. Pancreas International". Replies Morris.

"What were you doing at St. Pancreas International?" Asks Anthony.

"About to leave the country but changed my mind". Replies Morris, jokingly.

"Come on Morris - be serious". Says Anthony.

"Okay, just dropped Henrietta off, she is off to Paris". Says Morris.

"The Henrietta I met at Starbucks?" Asks Anthony.

"Yes". Says Morris.

"Has she gone for good?" Asks Anthony.

"No. just gone to Paris for a few days". Replies Morris.

"I am starving, do you fancy lunch?" Says Anthony.

"I could eat a horse right now". Says Morris.

"Not kidding, most meat right now contains horse DNA". Remarks Anthony.

"Just a figure of speech, do not take it that far". Says Morris.

"So, we'll meet at the usual place?" Says Anthony.

"See you in about forty minutes". Says Morris.

Morris starts his car and moves on. His phone rings again and he pulls over. It is Miah.

"How is your girlfriend, is she still with you?" Asks Miah.

"Did you say my girlfriend?" Morris enquires.

Miah giggles. "I know you too well Morris, I was just teasing," replies Miah.

"She is very beautiful and nice but it hasn't come to that yet," Morris retorts.

"I said, I was just teasing," says Miah, defensively.

"She has gone to Paris for a few days", says Morris, "By the way, I am going to the village restaurant to meet Anthony for lunch, would you care to join us?"

"Would love to". Replies Miah.

"Okay, be there in about forty minutes". Says Morris.

"Okay". Says Miah.

Morris continues driving, this time taking all the short cuts he could recognise, and within forty minutes he is at the village restaurant and is heading to the car park when Anthony pulls in and parks beside Morris's car. They walk into the restaurant and are seated at a table for three. The waitress makes her way to their table clutching a couple of menus.

Hello gentlemen, would you care to go to the other table which is for two, Asks waitress.

Just at that moment Miah walks in.

Morris says to the waitress, "Thank you very much but we are three". He indicates Miah who walks directly to their table and joins them.

Waitress with a smile says "I see, I will go and fetch one more menu".

She trots off and fetches another menu and leaves it on the table.

Anthony is pleasantly surprise to see Miah who he has developed a great interest in. Unsure of how she knew of his lunch meeting with Morris. Morris recognising the apparent surprise in Anthony's face, says to Anthony,

"I asked her to join us for lunch".

"Great, I was thinking perhaps that you are telepathic as well." Says Anthony sarcastically.

In the restaurant, a blonde-haired man of about fifty is dressed up in a long gown; the transvestite is also made up with red lip stick and artificial breasts. He has his back to the dining tables, unaware of the customers. He is talking to a couple of ladies sitting at the far side towards the wall. Morris is the only brown-coloured gentleman in the restaurant. The transvestite is sort of talking a lot and loudly to his two friends, oblivious of the presence of Morris, or indeed anyone else. He is describing a football match which took place in one of the east European countries, in which there was anti-semitic chant directed at some of the ethnic minority players in the away team. He seems to be enjoying his shenanigan in support of the chant. Customers are aware of the negative implications and genuinely displeased at the distasteful comments, but felt powerless to stop him.

Transvestite says to his friends, "I will be going to watch the next match and I will be wearing a monkey suit and probably will be eating bananas as well."

Most of the customers, including Anthony and Miah are visibly very uncomfortable at the transvestite's flippancy. There is complete silence, except for the voice of the transvestite who is carried away with his antics and not realising the bad feeling he is causing behind him, as he has his back to everyone except the two ladies he is talking to.

At this stage, Anthony who at this point is infuriated, gets up to challenge the transvestite but Morris gently pulls him back to his seat.

Morris gently gets up from his seat, and calmly walks up behind the transvestite and taps him on the shoulder from the back. As the transvestite turns, he is terrified to see Morris and he realises that all eyes are on him. At this point, one could hear a pin drop.

Morris sternly looks him directly in the eye.

"How old are you?" Asks Morris.

Transvestite panics and replies "Fifty".

"That's very silly indeed," Morris says, "You are fifty, and in fifty years you cannot work out whether you are a man or a woman."

There is thunderous laughter from the customers.

Morris continues, "I will advise you to wear a monkey suit next time". He looks at the Transvestite from head to toe, "because it will no doubt look better than this awful rag that is hanging on you".

On this note, all the customers erupt in laughter and cheer Morris. The restaurant manager goes to the front door, and holds it open and asks the transvestite to leave immediately and never to come back.

Morris, who is calmly composed, walks back to his table as the customers start to give him thumbs-up, but he remains indifferent and not carried away by the praise.

"Woah! I like your style Morris. I wish I could do that. You blatantly destroyed him with your mouth without touching him", says Anthony.

"The man needs help," says Morris, "and I am deeply compassionate of him. Evil comes from one's mouth and destroys one, whilst noble acts come from the heart and makes one worthy of respect. As you can see, it is not what he is wearing or his general make-up that prompted the incident – it was his utterances that provoked it and that was the only way I could stop him because he was causing uneasiness in everyone".

"When you rose from your seat and started to walk towards him, I honestly thought you were going to punch him". Says Miah.

"That is not necessary, the tongue is the deadliest weapon. Violence breads violence and does not win battles. Wisdom and inner fortitude engulfs one with honour". Says Morris.

When the dust settles, they start to look at the menu and invite the waitress to take their orders.

Waitress goes over to their table after taking the orders she says, "I am really glad that it turned out that way, the transvestite has been here a couple of times before and in each occasion he would make anti-semitic references which he seemed to enjoy, causing a lot of discomfort to our customers".

She takes the orders and leaves.

Morris tells Miah and Anthony that he will be having a party in a few days' time and would like them to be at the party.

"What is the party for?" Asks Anthony.

"For Henrietta, of course," Miah cuts in.

"No, it is for someone I met a few days ago. His name is Isabbul, he does not know the party is for him. I told him it is for a friend of mine whose birthday was on the first of April. I said this because he had earlier told me his birthday was on that date". Says Morris.

"I really care less who the party is for. I just want to party". Says Anthony.

"Me too". Says Miah.

She rises from her seat clutching her bag.

Anthony says to Miah, "You are not leaving yet, you have not had your meal".

"Just going to the powder room". Says Miah.

She leaves.

Anthony says to Morris, "You know I have always fancied Miah but the trouble is, she does not know that and I know she does not fancy me."

"Why are you so sure?" Asks Morris.

"You would know if a woman fancied you, wouldn't you?" Replies Anthony.

"So you know the mind of a woman, do you?" Asks Morris.

"Yes, sort of"…, replies Anthony.

"Show me a man who says he knows the minds of women or men and I will call him a liar" says Morris, The Daishonin says, "If you look into your mind, you will see nothing – is it red, blue, white or dark, or is it square, round or triangular; in other words, it has no colour or shape and yet you will not say it does not exist for many differing thoughts are born from it. It has the properties of existence and non-existence. Therefore, if you cannot perceive your own mind, how can you perceive someone else's mind? So, it is an illusive reality just like life itself." Anthony is now deep in thought as a result of The Daishonin's quote. There is complete silence.

"Do you know, it is so philosophical and true, I have not thought of it like that". Says Anthony.

"Why don't you tell her you fancy her?" Asks Morris, "You may be pleasantly surprised if you tell her."

"I can't do that". Replies Anthony.

"Why not?" Asks Morris.

"I suppose it is because my parents never told me that they loved me and during my time at boarding school, no one had said that to me, so it is not intrinsic in my nature." Replies Anthony defensively.

"But now you are a grown man, you can change all that". Says Morris.

"Yeah, pigs might fly…backwards". Says Anthony.

The waitress arrives with their order and serves them.

A few minutes later, Miah returns from the powder room and re-joins them as they tuck in to the sumptuous meal.

Anthony picks up a glass of water and is sipping it when unexpectedly Morris says to Miah, "Anthony fancies you."

To which Miah replies, "He's never told me that."

Anthony is embarrassed and instantly loses his grip on the glass of water and drops it, splashing water all over the table. The waitress comes over with a cloth and wipes the table dry again.

"Thank you". Anthony says to waitress, "Can you get the bill please?"

The waitress leaves and returns to say that the manager does not want them to pay for their meal.

"Why?" Asks Anthony.

"He said to tell you that it is on the house. Perhaps it is because of how he was helped to get rid of the transvestite". Replies waitress.

"I did not react just because he was a transvestite; it is simply that he was making a lot of people uncomfortable with his very ancient juvenile views. It was the only way to stop him". Morris explains.

"He understands that". Says waitress.

"I happen to know some transvestites who do not share his views and I do get on reasonably well with them". Remarks Morris.

They get up to leave; Morris walks up to the manager and thanks him for his hospitality and understanding;

The Manager also thanks Morris and tells him that the transvestite was completely out of order.

They leave the restaurant and make their way to the car park. As Morris is getting in his car he says to Anthony, "Would you give Miah a lift, I am going shopping." He then drives off.

Anthony is thinking whether that was Morris's plan to get him and Miah closer together; the same thought goes through Miah's mind. As Morris did not give them time to respond, it seems there is no way out, especially for Anthony who desperately wishes to avoid the idea. Maybe through women's intuition, Miah recognises that he is uncomfortable and she decides to take a bus to the town centre, but Anthony does not insist to give her a lift. On the bus she constantly thinks whether Anthony does not like her or simply that he is shy. Morris drives directly to a shop that sells musical instruments. The shop is adorned with different types of guitars. He is walking round and meticulously examining the guitars one after another. He is not a novice where guitars are concerned. He can play the guitar as well as the keyboard, which he learnt in his earlier years; he has also promoted some up and coming pop bands. Considering that these experiences were culti-vated a long time ago, he can still strum a few cords and has an ear for good music. It stems from when he used to audition, rehearse and find venues for pop groups to play. He is quite capable of spotting talent.

As he is curiously looking at several guitars, the shop assistant approaches him and asks if he could help.

Morris instantly asks, "Which of these guitars would you recommend for a professional"?

The shop assistant replies, "Indeed our guitars are mainly for professionals it just depends on choice and of course affordability; as you can see they have various price tags."

Morris, picking one of the guitars up says, "I like this one but the price is extortionate. It's alright, though, I'll take it."

"It is my favourite because it is versatile. It is excellent for any musician, be they professional or not, as it serves all purposes," replies the assistant.

Morris pays for the guitar and takes it away.

He moves on to a fashion shop and buys a checked shirt and blue jeans.

Chapter 10

Four days later, he receives a phone call from Henrietta, informing him that she is returning to the UK that evening by Eurostar. So he promises that he would pick her up from St. Pancreas International station. In the afternoon of the same day, he goes to number fifty-one; the elderly lady's house, to see if there were any letters.

He finds a post card addressed to him from the elderly lady, telling him that she would be returning to the UK in three days' time.

Morris sits down at the bottom of the stairs wondering why she sent the post card meant for him at her home address when she knew his home address. He finds it uncanny, could it be that she wanted to know if he actually visits her house as he promised her, perhaps using some of her investigative training acquired during the war? Maybe there is still a lot he needs to find out about her and determines to do that when she returns. He opens the front door and walks out, locking it behind him. As he starts heading back to his house he periodically glances at the post card, while still deep in thought.

Morris arrives at his house and picks his phone up and calls the arrival enquiries desk at Gatwick Airport to find out when the flight from Israel would be due to land in three days' time. He is informed that there would be only one flight due on that day which would be in the evening, at 5.30pm.

The elderly lady did not ask Morris for a lift, neither did she state the time of her arrival on the post card, but she is old and not quite fit to travel on her own.

She is not the type that likes to spend money on taxis which means that she would take the underground or buses instead, because of her pensioner status. Morris decides that he will go to pick her up from the airport on that day. Nevertheless, he cannot help thinking that she is quite stubborn.

However, he is pleased that both Henrietta and the elderly lady would be back in time for the party the following Saturday, although he is unsure if the elderly lady would attend.

In the evening, he drives to St. Pancreas International to collect Henrietta. When he gets to the car park he looks around for Kevin, the tramp that was kicking his dog because of some sausage rolls. His mattress is in the same position but Kevin is not there. So Morris parks his car and goes to the arrivals and checks the time. He is thirty minutes early so he waits around and goes back to the car park to look for Kevin, but to no avail, then he returns to the arrivals again and waits.

A few minutes later, the Eurostar from Paris roars in to the station and not long after that Henrietta emerges, clutching her small suitcase. She hurries up to Morris and kisses him passionately; he is also equally responsive. They make their way straight to the car park.

It is a delightful surprise when he sees Kevin with his dog. Kevin is looking very tired so Morris approaches him.

"Hello Kevin" says Morris.

Kevin gives Morris a passing gaze and then puts his carrier bag down and starts to unpack his food stuff, which comprises of half-eaten burgers, fries and some tins half-full of coke, expired packets of biscuits and some slices of bread. They stand watching him unpacking.

Henrietta says to Morris, "He does not recognise you".

"I am sure he does, he is just very tired," says Morris. Kevin raises his head and gazes at Morris again and smiles

"Gimme a cigarette – guv," says Kevin.

"Do you remember, I do not smoke, so I don't have a cigarette." Replies Morris.

"You're alright. Thanks again for the money". Says Kevin.

"Listen Kevin, I want you to come to my house on Saturday. We will have something to eat, a lot to drink and I will give you some cigarettes". says Morris.

Kevin looks certainly bewildered with mixed feelings, since no one has ever bothered to speak to him, let alone invite him for a meal, drink and some cigarettes. However, getting such an invitation from a total stranger seems far from reality. Nevertheless, this same person did care for him and his dog, by rescuing the dog when he was kicking at him; and to crown it all, he also gave Kevin a tenner to buy some sausages for himself and his dog. It is a tantalising offer for Kevin.

"Where do ya live, guv?" Asks Kevin.

"Never mind where I live. I will pick you up and bring you back". Says Morris.

"Who's gonna look after me dog then?" Asks Kevin.

"Bring your dog". Replies Morris.

"What day is it today?" Asks Kevin.

"It's Tuesday", replies Morris, "and I will pick you up on Saturday morning. I'll bring you some clean clothes in case you are worried about what to wear. You've got to be here so that I can find you – alright?"

Kevin responded with a nod of his head.

Morris searches his wallet and finds a twenty pound note; the only money in his wallet, and hands it over to Kevin.

"Use this for some sausages and some cigarettes and I will see you on Saturday morning."

Kevin takes the money and is dumbfounded to find a twenty pound note resting in his hand. For years he's never seen any paper money, except the ten pound note that Morris gave him earlier. He is gobsmacked.

Morris leaves with Henrietta and heads to his parked car. Kevin is still holding the twenty pound note in his hand, gazing at Morris in an unbelievable and dream-like state. Morris and Henrietta get in the car and drive off. There is silence for about ten minutes.

Morris then turns to Henrietta.

"How was your journey?" Morris asks Henrietta.

"Nothing much, my friend's auntie who leaves in Paris thinks my nan may still be here in London. She is an elderly lady of about eighty-six and had been in the Second World War. She did not stop talking about the war, and it was very boring". Replies Henrietta.

"Why did she think your nan could be in London?" Asks Morris,

"Because according to her", says Henrietta, "most of the women with whom she was associated during the war are residing in London. She meant those who were still alive ten years ago, so I am none the wiser. It is back to the drawing board I'm afraid".

"We will find her", He assures her.

"Do you know, somehow I believe you - whole heartedly". Says Henrietta.

Why did you give the tramp the only money in your wallet?

"He really needs it. That's why".

"Do you not need it?" Asks Henrietta.

"He needs it a lot more than I do. He is quite an elderly man. Do you expect him to go and get a job? He is a very brave man, constantly battling the daily onslaught of all sorts of weather conditions in that open car park without much food to fuel him".

"You are right, it must be lonely for him out there, he could not tell which day it is". Says Henrietta.

"I suppose there is nothing for him to look forward to, and yet he is pure gold in a rag bag". Says Morris.

Henrietta steals a wondrous gaze at Morris, indicating she did not understand what gold and a rag bag have to do with the tramp. It is evident that the statement did not make any sense to her. Morris certainly realises that but refuses to show it.

"Do you know," continues Morris, "when he asked what day it was – memories came flooding back of an incident in Raynes Park."

"What incident?" Asks Henrietta.

Morris replies, "One autumn evening, I was visiting a friend, so I parked my car in the street and as I kept walking down to my friend's house, I heard a very weak and feeble voice calling out, 'Young man.' I turned round, looked everywhere but could not see anyone. So I continued, and the voice called out again, this time with a sense of desperation, 'Young man! Young man!' I then stopped and took a few steps backwards and looked at every door in the direction of the voice, and suddenly I noticed a door which was ajar by about six inches".

Henrietta is curious, "And what happened?"

"I went closer to the door and saw a face peering through the gap from behind the door. She was an elderly lady, frail and thin. So, I stood right in front of the door and said, "Hello", can I help you" to which she replied, "What day is it?" So, I told her what day it was and asked her if she needed some help. She blanked me and quickly shut the door. I stood there wondering how I could help her because obviously she needed some help". Says Morris.

"And what happened then?" Asks Henrietta.

Morris continues, "So, I called the social services department and it went straight to the answer phone. I recorded a message telling them exactly what happened and emphasised that she may need urgent attention and care. I left her address and my phone number, should they wish to contact me".

"Did they contact you?" Asks Henrietta.

"No! Morris exclaims, "Sometimes I wonder how many people like her are lonely and need care and attention".

Later, they come to a crossroad and Morris veers in an unlikely direction. He notes that Henrietta is surprised at the turning he's made and before she can say any word or ask any questions, he explains to her that they are going to the doctor's surgery. She glances at him questioningly, as if to say, "what's the matter, are you suddenly unwell?"

Morris captures her thought and, says, "It's because of the party on Saturday, first of April. I am going there to give them an invitation."

"So the party is still on for real?" Asks Henrietta.

"Of course it is on. Surprised?" Replies Morris.

"Yes, you are simply mad" Henrietta says, "I mean that as a compliment".

"Why?" Asks Morris.

"Shouldn't I be? A party on the first of April; I was wondering if it was an April fool's type of party that will never materialise". Replies Henrietta.

Morris tells her emphatically that the party is for real.

They pull up in front of the doctor's surgery. It is the same surgery where Morris collected a prescription for the elderly lady. He gets out of the car while Henrietta remains in her seat. He walks directly to the reception and meets the same receptionist who attended to him last time. She was excited at seeing him again. Morris notices that there are only a handful of patients this time around.

"Good to see you again, Morris". Says Receptionist.

"I popped in to give you an invitation to my party on Saturday," says Morris.

"This Saturday?" Asks Receptionist.

"Yes, this Saturday, first of April. Replies Morris.

"Are you sure it is not an April fool's party?" Asks Receptionist.

"Nothing like that." Says Morris.

Morris hands three invitation cards to the receptionist.

"One for you, one for the doctor and one for any patient who wishes to come, especially any of those that were here on my previous visit". Says Morris.

Receptionist accepts the invitation cards and is excited for being invited. She says to Morris "I am sure they will all want to come to your party. count me in, I will be there for sure".

Morris leaves the surgery and hurries back to the car to find Henrietta deep in focus and silently chanting some phrase inaudibly.

Morris witnessing that, asks Henrietta, "What are you mumbling with such an intense concentration?"

"Do you know, since that morning that you performed your ceremony in your house, I really, really enjoyed that chant. It was so powerful a sound and positively soothing that I have been chanting the same ever since, whenever I am alone". Replies Henrietta.

"What exactly were you chanting?" Asks Morris.

"The same phrase that you chanted during your 'ceremony' as you called it." Replies Henrietta.

Henrietta repeats the chant to Morris.

Morris is delightfully surprised at her remark and nods affirmatively.

With emphasis, Morris exclaims, "Excellent! *That* is the sound of the sun, this is the evidence that when one seeks with one's heart, one will definitely find. You've got it!"

"What's next or is that all?" asks Henrietta, "I recollect that you also did a bit of recitation in a foreign language".

Morris begins to explain, "That's right. It is a mixture of classical Chinese and Sankrit. The chant is the primary practice; the recitation may take you a little time, so, in the meantime keep chanting the one essential phrase and your life is bound to turn three hundred and sixty degrees towards happiness, peace and realisation of your desires as you take action. That phrase deepens, strengthens and enriches your life, purifying your five senses of sight, smell, touch, taste and hearing. They are the five sensory organs with which you perceive your environment. Essentially, when we manifest the life of this phrase in ourselves, we will be able to make everything in the universe function for our benefit."

"Everything?" Asks Henrietta.

"Yes, definitely everything, it is the one essential law of cause and effect, the ultimate law of life and the universe". Says Morris.

"Woah!" exclaims Henrietta, "That is powerful. So, that's why *you* are - the way you are?"

"Everyone, and I mean, everyone, can manifest his or her own intrinsic qualities when he or she makes this law the basis of their life. Positive qualities are heightened and negative ones are transformed and also begin to create value". Says Morris.

"I am very happy to have met you." says Henrietta.

"It's no coincidence that we met, nothing ever is, anyway". Morris remarks.

"It is my wish to meet my nan, and I hope it will be fulfilled".

"Let it be. Just keep chanting the essential phrase, with faith". Says Morris.

"I recognise that song, It is by...John Lennon. Can you sing it?" Says Henrietta.

Morris bursts into his characteristic and infectious laughter. Henrietta cannot help it but falls about laughing too.

"I was not talking about the song". Says Morris, "I simply meant that if your desire was to find your nan, "let it be". It is just a figure of speech which in that context means "may your wishes be realised".

Chapter 11

In the evening of Friday, the day the elderly lady informed Morris on a post card that she would be returning from Israel, Morris drives to Gatwick Airport in the off-chance that she would arrive as she said. On the way to the airport, wandering thoughts get the better of him, as the elderly lady did not request a lift from him and she did not mention the time of her flight's arrival. Did she want him to come to pick her up from the airport, if so, why did she not mention it? He does not know whether she would be coming back alone or with some-one. Would she appreciate him just turning up at the airport uninvited just to give her a lift home? After all he does not really know her that well but because he feels empathy towards her, his determination does not wane in his effort to help her. After a lot of contemplation however, he is convinced he is doing the right thing.

By this time he is already in the airport's car park. Confidently he strolls into the arrival terminal and starts milling around, reading the information on the screen with the intention of finding out if the elderly lady's flight had arrived or is about to arrive. He notices that the flight arrived thirty minutes earlier and is delighted. He goes across to the information desk to learn that customs and immigration checks would take about thirty minutes before the first passenger appears in the arrival lounge, so, he takes an inconspicuous position to wait for her with his eyes fixed at the arrival gate. He does not want her to see him first.

He must have been waiting for about fifty minutes when the elderly lady appears, dragging her small suitcase along when, suddenly, a gentleman wearing a three piece suit trips over her suitcase and lands on the floor.

The elderly lady is not pleased that he's disturbed her movement and she starts to hit him with her little handbag, adding to his embarrassment. The gentleman picks himself up, stares at her in apparent bewilderment and walks off.

Morris begins to wonder whether the elderly lady's eccentricity was a derivative of her training during the war. She continues walking along and Morris sneaks out from where he is standing and follows her; she has not seen him. She goes out to the taxi rank and starts to search her wallet. After a while, she heads off towards the train station and just as she is about to enter, Morris, who is about two metres behind her, says, "Hello".

She stops, turns round and sees Morris who is calmly approaching her. At this time Morris notices a deep sense of relief in her persona. It is only at this point that he feels confident to interact with her, knowing very well that she will appreciate a lift. He relieves her of her little suitcase and changes direction towards the car park and without hesitation she follows him.

"You look tired, Dr. Bozivich". Remarks Morris

"I did not tell you what my name was, where did you get it from?" Asks Dr Bozivich.

"Your GP called you by that name, when I collected your prescription". Morris explains defensively.

"Thank you for sending them, they were gladly received." Says Dr. Bozivich.

"How was your holiday?" Asks Morris.

"Okay," says Dr. Bozivich, "my friend, Isabella, and I chatted till three o'clock in the morning most of the time, in reminiscent of our covert activities during the war. She was a very good spy, although she thinks I was a better spy than she was. On the whole, we played our parts very well indeed".

Her face lights up with apparent satisfaction.

"Do you regret any of the things you did during that war?" Asks Morris.

"Yes, just one thing", Replies Dr. Bozivich, "I fell in love with an ordinary soldier on guard at a nuclear facility station."

"I do not think that falling in love deserves regret," Says Morris, "No one knows who he or she is going to fall in love with or when one is going to fall in love. It just happens and it is uncontrollable. It can't be true love if you knew with whom or when you will fall in love".

"I suppose so, the trouble is that I had his baby..." says Dr. Bozivich regretfully.

"Boy or girl?" Asks Morris.

"Girl, and he did not know I was a spy," replies Dr. Bozivich, "That's the way it was. I really used him to get some vital information for the opposite side – resulting in the annihilation of that nuclear facility that he guarded, with a single bomb".

They get to Morris's car, get in and Morris drives off. There is complete silence. Morris is wondering whether the baby is still alive, and if she is, why is Dr. Bozivich alone and in a state of complete neglect?

Suddenly Dr. Bozivich sighs with a deep sense of regret.

"Where is your family young man?" Asks Dr. Bozivich.

"I have two children, both grown up. They went through university and they are here in London. I was divorced from their mother because of some trivial incidents, like arguing in the presence of the children. Initially it was acrimonious, but right now it is far from that. We are good friends and the children are happy with that, although they are no longer children now." Replies Morris.

"It's best not to stay in an unhappy marriage just for the sake of the children", Says Dr. Bozivich, "in an unhappy marriage, children tend to absorb negative vibrations from such an environment, they are affected by it adversely and can reflect in their character".

"I think it's best not to course unhappiness in one's marriage in the first place. Unfortunately, it all happened before I graduated in the art-of-living". Says Morris.

"The art of what?" Asks Dr. Bozivich.

"Living," ... "I make the sound of the sun, which I was completely ignorant of before, and during the marriage. As a result, my negative karma got the worst of me. Since I started making the sound of the sun, I am in control of what I say, think and do". Replies Morris.

"It sounds good". Says Dr. Bozivich.

"So, one becomes the master of one's life". Says Morris.

"For some reason, I believe you completely". Adds Dr. Bozivich.

"I find it strange that you believed me without needing any explanation". Says Morris.

"That's simple, I can see the truth of what you say in your life. That's why I believe you...because you are that truth." Replies Dr. Bozivich.

As Morris keeps driving, there is silence as conversation stops. Morris is now faced with several thoughts conflicting in his mind; wondering what could have happened to the baby girl Dr. Bozivich had with the soldier she fell in love with. If that baby is still alive, Dr. Bozivich probably would be a grandmother. He does not ask in case it triggers some bad memories for her.

They reach her house in Wimbledon and Morris parks the car, helps her get out of the car and rushes to the front door and opens it. Dr. Bozivich slowly enters, while Morris follows. She stands behind the door meticulously scanning the whole interior. Morris is standing behind her, unsure why she is sort of examining the whole house. Could she be thinking that perhaps Morris used the house in her absence for some sort of shenanigan, or could she be thinking that some of the furniture could be missing or whether they are in the right places as she left them?

However, after careful examination she makes her way to the small room close to the kitchen and falls into bed, apparently tired from her journey from Israel. Morris excuses himself and goes outside, shutting the front door behind him. He gets into his car and drives off. Dr. Bozivich is too tired to ask him where he is going as she is relieved to be alone. She closes her eyes and falls asleep.

Morris is now in the Indian takeaway, perusing the menu. He dials some numbers but does not get through, so he orders some conventional cuisine, comprising of rice and fish source, which is not too spicy. He hopes that it will do nicely.

He feels sympathetic knowing that Dr. Bozivich might be very hungry since there is no food in her house, and grabs a couple of orange juice and hurries back to her house. Morris still has the keys she left with him before travelling to Israel, so he unlocks the front door and on entering he suddenly encounters a shoe ferociously flying towards him. As he ducks, it misses him by a couple of centimetres.

Morris collects himself from the surprisingly and unexpected incident, and stands still staring at Dr. Bozivich with jaw dropping bewilderment. She is sitting up in the bed with a combined rage and gladness in her face. Rage because she hates intruders and gladness because it is Morris – and she missed him.

"Very sorry young man," she says, "I really thought it was an intruder since I was not expecting you back now. I have never been known to miss my target, this is the first time and I am so glad I did."

Morris, who is speechless, slowly enters the small room where Dr. Bozivich is sitting upright in bed. He places the food and drink on the table and says, "I knew you would be hungry so I got these for you."

"Thank you young man, you read me correctly...I was starving. I could eat a horse now, including the rider" says Dr. Bozivich appreciatively.

"That's quite witty", says Morris.

He goes to the kitchen and finds a fork and knife and places them on the table. He steps back and sits down in a chair beside the table watching her transport the food into her mouth in large portions.

Morris is wondering how such an elderly lady could acquire such skill of using a shoe as a deadly weapon, executing the attack with such ferocious energy and precision. He couldn't wait to ask her but he decides to be patient until she finishes her meal. What if he had not ducked in time, perhaps he could have found himself in a hospital – that is in the best case scenario. He wonders if she had launches such an attack before, if she has, what would have been the result? If she is capable of executing such an attack at her age now, he wonders what she was capable of doing when she was a lot younger ... as a spy. Most probably she would have learnt that during the war.

No sooner did that thought cross his mind, than Dr. Bozivich places the cutlery on her plate which is now empty. She adjusts her sitting position and faces him.

"I enjoyed this meal young man," she says to Morris. "That is quite considerate of you."

"If I knew you would like it that much I would have got you much more, but when I tried to call you on my phone I could not get through," replies Morris.

Glancing at her antique telephone she says, "I haven't got a telephone, I disconnected my phone a while ago because I hardly ever used it. No one calls me so, there is no need having a telephone and paying for the sake of just having a phone." She continues, "Do you know ...I have not been to the upstairs of this house for three years, so, equally it might as well not been there."

"Why?" Morris asks.

"Because I fell over years ago coming down the stairs and bruised my lower leg; coupled with the fact that I have no need to go upstairs," she replies.

Morris stands up to leave.

"I will be having a little birthday party tomorrow evening and I hope you will be able to come," he asks enquiringly.

She hesitates for a while. "So it's your birthday?" She asks. "No, it is a friend's birthday but the party is at my house and I would like you to come." Morris insists.

"You only live down the road, so I would love to attend," Dr. Bozivich replies.

"OK, I will pick you up at 7pm," Morris says. He leaves, closing the door behind him.

Chapter 12

Party Preparations

It is seven O'clock on Saturday morning. Morris is awakened by the sound of his doorbell; he is not expecting anyone at that time of the morning, so he hurriedly puts on his pyjamas and heads to the front door and opens it. To his surprise, Anthony is standing there. Morris is about to ask some questions but Anthony walks passed him and enters. Morris follows reluctantly.

"The party is tonight, am I right?" Asks Anthony.

"Yes, in the evening and not early in the morning, Anthony". Replies Morris.

"I am aware of that, so I tried to surprise you." says Anthony

"You surely succeeded." Says Morris.

"Well, what are friends for. It is just to let you know that I have ordered all the drinks you may need – and a variety of Thai food. They will be delivered around 7pm. So make sure you are in to collect them". Instructs Anthony.

"Did you say you have already ordered them?" Asks Morris.

"Yes, ordered and paid for". Replies Anthony.

"Thank you very much indeed, but it is only a small party for a friend I don't even know. If you had let me know about that earlier I would have not let you order them". Says Morris.

Anthony is pleased because he has succeeded in getting his own way.

"That is exactly why I did not tell you about it because you would not accept, so, I did it my way" says Anthony. "You are always giving, now I am seizing this opportunity to give something to you and you can't stop me. By the way, is the party going to be held in your garden or indoors?"

"Both, it will spill over to the garden eventually". Replies Morris.

Anthony starts to leave and says to Morris,

"Great! It's good to know".

He closes the door behind him, gets in his car and speeds off.

Morris goes back to bed for a while, then gets up again, has a bath and goes to perform his ceremony (meditation and prayer). No sooner has he finished his ceremony than the telephone rings. He answers it; it is a local company. He learns that they are on their way to his house to prepare his garden. A Few minutes later, they arrive and start to facilitate and decorate Morris's garden with some colourful canopies and marquee, artificial plants and flowers.

Morris is just standing and watching the swift activity taking place. Though he did not ask for this work to be done, he has an idea that it could be Anthony who organised it. Within a short time the work is completed and the garden is completely transformed for the best. The entire garden is also wired for electric light.

The workmen start to leave and Morris remains overwhelmingly speechless. His phone rings again and this time it is Henrietta informing him that she is on her way with some girls from a local cleaning company. Morris quietly sits down on the sofa and starts to read a book; he did not read for long when Henrietta knocks on the front door. He goes to the door and opens it. Henrietta and three gorgeous girls in blue overalls are standing at the door. Before Morris could say "come in" Henrietta breezes passed him, followed by the three girls. Morris is still holding the door, dazed at what is happening.

Henrietta takes the lead, showing the girls the toilet, kitchen, the hallway, including the lounge. She asks them to clean and dust the entire place with exceptional excellence.

The girls are surprised because the whole house is clean and may not need cleaning. Morris believes in cleanliness and always keeps his house and his car in pristine condition. However, Morris does not utter a word but goes into the kitchen and puts the kettle on. Henrietta joins Morris in the kitchen.

He is silent but slowly walking closer to Henrietta and gives her a strong appreciative embrace.

"Cup of Tea?" Asks Morris.

Henrietta does not answer but holds on to the meaningful embrace with her head placed firmly to his chest and starts to speak softly as she sobs.

"Morris, please do not think it is out of character, it is just that you have been giving me everything and I have been thinking how I could return the kindness but do not know how. So, since you are having a party tonight, this is the only way I could contribute – to have your house in tip-top condition. Perhaps it is irrational, since you always keep your house clean but that's all I could think of." Pleads Henrietta.

Morris turns Henrietta's head to face him, holding it with both hands. He looks directly into her eyes appreciatively and kisses her on the mouth.

"That means a lot to me, it is thoughtful of you – thank you". says Morris

They separate from the embrace and he makes two cups of tea and hands one to her. He gently holds her by the hand and leads her to the lounge where they sit, drinking tea.

A few minutes later, the girls appear in the lounge. Henrietta begins to introduce the girls to Morris.

"This is Grace, Sharon and Paris. she turns to the girls, "Girls, this is Morris."

"You two have not been married for long, am I right?" Asks Grace

"Why?" Asks Morris.

"It is obvious, Is it not?" Says Sharon.

"You look so in love and contented and it does not happen to couples who have married for a long time – it is not rocket science". Says Paris.

"Thank you for your infallible observations", says Henrietta.

"I was married ones and all we succeeded in doing was pretend to be happy whenever friends or family came to see us, but we really hated each other's guts. Thank goodness it is over." Says Paris.

"It takes two to make a happy marriage and grass is not greener on the other side. You still have to water it." says Grace.

"I looked at your garden through the bathroom window and it looks so dapper, how come?" Remarks Paris.

Morris interrupts and asks Henrietta to tell them about the party.

Henrietta says to the girls, "Yes, there will be a party here tonight."

"And you are all invited." Says Morris.

"Really?" Asks Grace.

"Yes, really, we shall be expecting all of you". Replies Morris.

"Thank you". Says Sharon with excitement.

"What time does it start?" Asks Paris.

Morris informs them that it will start from 7.30pm.

Henrietta asks if they would like a cup of tea before they leave.

"No thanks, we are going to another job now." Says Grace.

The three girls leave.

Henrietta then asks Morris, "What was Sharon saying about your garden being dapper?"

"You should take a look at the garden" says Morris.

Henrietta goes into the kitchen and looks out at the garden. She is astonished but pleasantly surprised.

"When did you do all of this?" Henrietta asks.

"This morning," replies Morris. "credit to Anthony, he organised it all as a surprise and got a local company in. Just a couple of hours after that, you dropped your own bomb shell by bringing the girls in. I hope it did not cost you an arm and a leg hiring those girls to do the cleaning."

Henrietta gently stroking his hair and says, "I wish I could really give something to you, I mean something worthwhile."

"Come on, don't be silly, your genuine thoughtfulness means a lot to me," Morris retorts.

There is a brief silence.

"Do you ever wonder why total strangers always think we are married?" Asks Henrietta.

"It has not crossed my mind. Perhaps, they want us to get married". Says Morris.

Henrietta giggles.

There is a knock at the front door, Morris goes to open the door and his telephone starts to ring. He is opening the door while answering the phone at the same time. It was Anthony on the phone warning him that a van loaded with drinks is on its way to his house. As Morris opens the door there is a van outside his house. The driver asks Morris where to offload the drinks. He tells him to offload it in his garden, through the side door to the garden. He tells Anthony on the phone that the van is already at his house.

"Will the quantity be enough? Asks Anthony.

"A whole van load of drinks and you ask if it will be enough?" Morris replies with a concoction of sarcasm and gratitude.

"If anyone needs picking up or dropping off before or after the party, just let me know and I will gladly help out" says Anthony.

"Sure, I will," Morris says, and he returns to join Henrietta in the lounge.

She glances at her watch. "It is not lunch time yet and there has been a lot of activities already. I need to go to my flat and get changed before the party. On second thoughts, I'd rather stay for a while to give you a hand," says Henrietta.

There is another knock on the front door and Morris opens it – it is the van driver, he has completely offloaded the contents of his van and is about to depart. He could not help asking Morris if whatever party was going to take place that evening was a competition to find who is going to drink for England? Morris replies that it was intended to be a simple small party but it seems that some of his friends have other ideas. It sounds like a good Idea whatever their intentions are. Morris asks the van driver to attend the party if he wishes. The van driver accepts, and happily leaves. By this time Henrietta is busy in the garden placing the drinks on the tables, and the rest she places in large numbers in the four corners of the garden.

Morris picks up his phone and starts calling some of his friends who he had not told about the impending party, to invite them. He must have spent about an hour on the phone when Henrietta enters the lounge; she becomes aware of what Morris is doing, so decides not to disturb him. She goes back in the kitchen and begins to prepare some food. It is past lunch time when Morris eventually finishes making his calls. Just at that moment, Henrietta enters the lounge with a tray containing delicious cuisine and places it on Morris's lap.

Morris is utterly appreciative.

"That's excellent timing, I am starving. Where is yours?" Asks Morris.

Henrietta goes into the kitchen and brings her own tray and sits beside him. They tuck into the food with plenty of appetite.

"Do you not think it is too late to be inviting your friends to the party – should you not have done that sometime ago?" Asks Henrietta.

"It was not planned like this sometime ago, it was supposed to be a simple small gathering, so I invited a handful of people, but now the whole idea has trans-

formed, therefore, a large number of people is required".
Says Morris.

Henrietta is concerned that Morris's friends may not
be able to turn up because the invitation was impromptu.
However, Morris is confident that they will all turn up.

Henrietta does not doubt Morris, but she is a little
concerned, nevertheless she is overly interested to see
how it pans out. She decides to go home and change for
the party.

Late in the evening, a transit van from a catering
company delivers a variety of food; some hot meals and
some cold stuff, such as salads etc. There is more than
enough to go round.

The weather is beautiful; the sky is clear with numerous stars which seem to cast their bright lights directly
at Morris's garden. There is a gentle breeze which does
not beleaguer the leaves on the trees.

The first guest is Dr. Bozivich. She is leaning against
the patio doors admiring the exotic arrangement in the
garden and she is overwhelmed. Anthony arrives a few
minutes later, looking very happy and fulfilled at seeing
the magical opulence of Morris's garden which is largely
due to his sincere desire to contribute. He is satisfied
that he has been able to do something for Morris for a
change. Morris seems to be self-sufficient and gets on
considerably very well; forever helping and taking
others challenges as if they were his own. He is totally
selfless, always concerned for the happiness of others.
With these thoughts in mind, Anthony helps himself to
a glass of wine.

Morris comes out of his bedroom with a piece of
paper and hands it over to Anthony. He also gives him a
checked shirt and jeans for Kevin.

His name is Kevin and he lives in St. Pancreas International car park.

"Lives in the car park?" Asks Anthony, disgustingly.

"Yes, details are on this piece of paper' says Morris", He Indicates the piece of paper that he handed over to Anthony, "He is waiting to be collected and make sure he changes into the checked shirt and jeans.

Anthony takes the piece of paper from Morris, folds it and puts it in his top pocket and puts the bag with the shirt and jeans down by his side and continues drinking the glass of wine. He is not immensely surprised. He knows that Morris is totally oblivious to discrimination and does not judge anyone either. His friends are from various backgrounds irrespective of ethnicity, economic attainment or social status. He sees things differently. Anthony puts his glass of wine down and leaves.

Chapter 13

Around 8pm, more guests start to arrive in groups of twos, threes and fours, and within a short time the whole garden is almost filled. The atmosphere is quite friendly and lively as they mingle with each other with plates of food in every hand amid the soft background music.

Morris starts walking round, welcoming his guests and looking to see if Isabbul is amongst the crowd but there is no sign of him. A few minutes later, Henrietta arrives by taxi in front of the house. She settles her fare and as she proceeds towards the front door she notices a figure of a young man standing motionless by the door. She does not recognise who he was because it's dark. She ignores him and swiftly calls Morris on her phone to open the front door and let her in. Morris arrives within seconds and lets her in. He holds her hand and leads her directly to Dr. Bozivich, who is now sitting in a chair on the patio busily munching a leg of chicken; a large scotch is on the table beside her. Morris introduces Henrietta.

Henrietta takes a close look at Dr. Bozivich and says to Morris, "Is this the lady I met at the airport; she came to talk to me when you dropped her off, is she not?"

"That is correct," replies Morris.

Dr. Brosivich is feeling merrily; she has consumed a considerable amount of alcohol. Although she does not seem to be too drunk but she is certainly incapable of recognising anyone. She does not remember or recognise Henrietta, so, Morris and Henrietta begin to move on towards the garden.

"I saw a man standing motionless by your front door," says Henrietta.

"When?" asks Morris.

"When I called you to let me in," replies Henrietta.

They immediately turn round and quickly proceed to the front door. A figure is just walking away when Morris calls out, "Isabbul!"

Isabbul turns around and responds, "Hello Morris."

"Why didn't you come in?" asks Morris.

Isabbul says, "On seeing all these fancy cars outside, I guessed it would be quite intimidating for me to mix with the guests Morris."

Isabbul is wearing the same clothes as when Morris met him at the front door of a supermarket, begging. Morris puts his hands on Isabbul's shoulder and leads him into his front door, then to the kitchen where some of the food is laid out in buffet style.

"Help yourself to whatever you fancy, there is plenty of drink too," Morris tells Isabbul, who is completely taken aback at the large quantities and variety of food and drink available. He quickly grabs a plate and helps himself.

Morris and Henrietta join the guests in the garden and he starts to introduce Henrietta to them. She looks stunningly beautiful in a body hugging yellow cotton dress which nicely hugs her slim body, revealing her well-defined feminine contours which truly complement the colour of her dress. Her high-heeled shoes, which are designed in black and yellow leather, enable her to glide gracefully through the garden, from one group of Morris's friends to another.

A few minutes later, Morris leaves Henrietta with a group of his very close friends and goes back to the kitchen where he had left Isabbul.

By this time Isabbul has finished eating but resorts to sampling various wines. Morris gently drags him by the hand and they join Henrietta and his friends. The party is now in full swing; a lot of laughter and mingling are evident.

Suddenly, Anthony arrives with Kevin who is undoubtedly looking quite trendy in the checked shirt and designer jeans bought for him by Morris. Morris announces that he has something to say, so the chatting and mingling are slightly muted as the guests are curious to listen to what Morris is about to say.

"Ladies and gentlemen, the reason why we are all here tonight is because of this young man." Morris points at Isabbul. "It is in fact his birthday today, therefore, I invited all of you to wish him a happy birthday. He did not know before now that this party was indeed for him. It was supposed to be a surprise. So if we raise our glasses, we will toast for peace, good health and happiness."

Everyone raises their glass and toasts Isabbul's birthday.

Morris continues. "You can observe without a doubt that he has accumulated a lot of good fortune due to the causes he made in the past to attract this event, which is quite responsive. All of us here are from various countries and backgrounds but we are all here for the same purpose. As we can see, and what's more, we are all part of it indicating that humanity is more important than geography. The Buddha says, 'If you wish to know what causes you've made in the past, you should look at your life as it is in the present, and if you wish to know what your life will be like in the future – you should look at the causes you are making now.'"

There is a loud cheer from the guests. Morris swiftly trots into the house and returns clutching a beautiful guitar which he bought earlier from the shop and gives it to Isabbul.

"He told me he lost his guitar, so I got one for him as a present and I hope he will make good use of it."

Isabbul is lost for words as he admires his new guitar, and then stares into the crowd and bursts out crying; tears begin to roll down his cheeks. Henrietta finds some tissues and wipes his tears. He sits on the grass cross-legged – right on the spot where he was standing, patiently tuning the guitar, string by string oblivious to the surrounding and the presence of the entire guests.

Then without warning, preparation or much ado, he starts to play classically and then some blues and rock, softly at first then gradually reaching a crescendo. The guests are gobsmacked as they begin to drift closer and closer almost in a circle around Isabbul. There is total silence, except for the sound of his guitar piercing through the night's gentle breeze. If not for the sound of his music one could hear a pin drop. Isabbul is now totally consumed in his music, while the guest are completely absorbed, listening to the clear sound of his guitar-playing and his electrifying vocals, which resounds in a magical and profound harmony.

Isabbul reaches a crescendo and goes straight to playing,

You are wonderful tonight,

originally by Eric Clapton, although, in parts he changes the words to suit, as he dedicates the song to Morris and Henrietta.

When he finally finishes this song he looks up to the guests; his entire performance must have lasted an hour or more non-stop, during which everyone was captivated. The guests begin to cheer for about five minutes.

One of Morris's friends, Alan, hastily approaches Morris and asks,

"Where did you find this guy - Morris"?

"In front of a supermarket begging for some money to buy something to eat," replies Morris.

"He is a rare gem", says Alan, "I have been in the music industry as producer/director for twenty years but never have I come across someone who plays the guitar and sings like he does; he is incredible. Do you mind if I work with him?"

Morris says to Alan, "Ask him, I am sure he wants to work as long as it is playing the guitar."

Chapter 14

The following morning, Morris takes Henrietta to the woods where they had been once before. The charms of the woods remain, portraying the same magical ambiance as previous.

She says to Morris, "One of your friends at the party told me of your experience in New York a long time ago. He said you fell head over heels in love with a girl you met on the subway, and when you went to pick her up for a night-out you found her unconscious in her apartment."

"That is correct, replies Morris, she was a pretty young girl and I would not let her out of my sight without talking to her. So I approached her, and we had a joyful chat; what's more, she accepted my invitation to take her out the same evening but it turned out to be a total disaster. It was love at first sight, unfortunately it was not meant to be. I still think of her sometimes".

"I had a similar experience when I lived in New York. I got off the train in the subway when this guy approached me, for some unknown reason we had a joyful conversation and, believe me, I fell in love with him right there and then, which is uncharacteristic of me. He was going to pick me up from my apartment for a night-out but I never saw him again". Says Henrietta.

"So he did not turn up then". Asks Morris.

"I cannot say because I woke up in a hospital the following day". Replies Henrietta.

Morris is thoughtful for a while, and gazes into Henrietta's eyes and says, "very uncanny; both of our experiences were to do with the subway in New York. What were you in hospital for?" He asks.

"The doctor told me that the police found a syringe stuck in my arm, so they suspected drug overdose and I was unconscious when they came into my apartment so I was rushed to the hospital where I woke up the following day." Says Henrietta.

"Drug overdose?" Asks Morris.

Henrietta giggles and says, "That was not the case. Do you remember the little girl I was playing with at the beach in Australia the first time I saw my nan?" She asks Morris.

"Yes", Replies Morris, "that was the time your nan had that ugly encounter with your mum?"

"Yes, she is grown up now and lives in New York. She was chronically anaemic and had various syringes for injecting herself when her blood sugar was low. She came to see me at the apartment that morning and left her syringes on a small table in my apartment and we went shopping but she forgot to collect them. When I got home in the evening, I noticed she had forgotten them so, I picked up one of them and then as I began to look at it the telephone suddenly rang. I suspected it would be her. I panicked and leaned forward to pick up the phone; the syringe I was holding in my hand accidentally got stuck in my arm. On seeing it stuck in my arm I fell back on the settee and passed out. The police thought that all the syringes were some kind of drug fixation apparatus but the result of their investigation was to the contrary."

Morris is speechless for a while; he is just standing and gazing intently at Henrietta. He is deep in thought.

"Which part of New York did this take place – Queens?" Asks Morris.

"Queens." Replies Henrietta.

They both mention 'Queens' at the same time.

Morris continues, "An apartment in Woodstock Avenue?"

Henrietta is astonished. She steps forward and so does Morris. They hug each other in a very tight embrace and hold it tighter and tighter. It is a magical moment.

"I was the prince that came to take you out for the evening. I was also the one that called the police. I just wanted you saved, so I phoned the police and disappeared and have been thinking about you since then". Says Morris.

"Deep down I expected to meet you again, someday", says Henrietts, "You have not been out of my mind since. You have changed a little, your hair – and you have got bigger."

"So have you", says Morris, "I was going to come back for you after that incident but I was only on a short visit to New York then. I left two days later for London. It is said that when one makes the sound of the sun all one's good fortune will be restored...*this* is a fine example."

Morris gently detaches himself from the tight embrace, kneels down in front of her and proposes,

"I want you to be my wife, will you marry me?"

Henrietta jumps up in esthetical joy "Yes! Yes! Yes!" She replies.

Morris gets up and kisses her on the cheek and they hurry out of the woods holding hands and are very happy as if they were two little children who have just discovered that they had received their ideal presents for Christmas.

Chapter 15

Two weeks later, Morris arrives home to find a piece of paper that had been dropped through the letterbox by Dr. Bozivich, asking him to come over to her house as soon as possible. Morris reads the note, shuts the door behind him and goes directly to her house.

He goes to the small room by the kitchen where she is lying down in bed.

"Sit down my son," Dr. Bozivich says to Morris.

He drifts to the chair by the table opposite the bed and sits down. He begins to gaze at two paintings leaning against the bed, and an enlarged photograph placed on the table. He wonders why she has displayed them. Several thoughts are going through his mind, while Dr. Bozivich is struggling to sit up on the bed. At last she sits up and picks up the paintings with both hands and gives them to him. Morris examines the paintings puts them aside and thanks her with a gentle and appreciative smile.

"They are beautiful". Says Morris.

"I know you will like them – I noticed you like beautiful things". Says Dr. Bozivich.

Morris points at the enlarged picture in a frame on the table and asks, "Who is that"?

"My daughter, Amanda," she replies. "Amanda lives in Australia."

"Has she ever been to the UK – to see you?" Asks Morris.

"Just once, about fifteen years ago, and she's never been back since." She replies'

"Do you have her phone number?"

"Her number and address are at the back of the frame."

Morris lifts the picture and takes out the phone number and the address.

"Will it be okay if I call her sometime?" Morris asks.

Dr. Bozivich asks Morris to call her daughter whenever he wants. She adds that Amanda is now divorced and that she used to teach dancing in a local school in Western Australia.

Morris notices that Dr. Bozivich looks a little frail and weak. Her voice is not as strong as it is used to be.

"You look tired, are you well?" He asks.

"No son, that's why I asked you to come over as soon as possible".

"What is the matter?" He asks.

"You have to call an ambulance; I need to go into hospital". She replies.

Morris immediately starts to key in the hospital number on his phone. Dr. Bozivich gestures to him not to.

Dr. Bozivich insists, "Son, not now. You must not call an ambulance right now. You must wait until after 12 midnight to call.

"Why?" Asks Morris.

"At that time my neighbours would have gone to bed, I don't want them to see an ambulance in front of my house". Replies Dr. Bozivich.

"In that case, I have to pop back to my house and take care of a couple of things. I will be back at midnight – is that alright?" Says Morris.

"That's fine", says Dr. Bozivich.

"In the meantime, try and put some clean clothes in a small suitcase, should you have to be admitted for a day or two in the hospital". Says Morris.

"I will do that son. See you a bit later".

Morris takes the two paintings and leaves.

When he gets to his house, he stands for a while deep in thought, then sits down on his sofa, retrieves Amanda's telephone number to call her but then on second thought decides not to.

Before he saw Dr. Bozivich's note asking him to come as soon as possible, he had taken Henrietta out for a meal and dropped her off at her flat. During that meal she told him that her contract for the flat runs out that very day and that the landlord would come to see her that evening to let her know if she could extend the contract. Morris was just about to call her when Henrietta calls and tells him that the landlord called her to say that he would see her the following day. This means that she would not know if her contract for the flat was still valid.

Morris told her he has just returned from Dr. Bozivich and that he would be going back again to get her an ambulance at 12. midnight, as she is not very well. There is a pause. Morris asks why the silence. Henrietta replies that if Dr. Bozivich is not well, why would he get the ambulance at 12 midnight, why not get her the ambulance immediately. Morris told her that Dr. Bozivich specifically wanted him to wait until 12 midnight.

At 12 midnight, Morris walks over to Dr. Bozivich's house. She has already packed some clothes in a small suitcase ready for the ambulance. Morris calls the hospital and is told that the ambulance would be there in a few minutes. About forty minutes later, there is a knock at the front door – as she never has visitor, it is obvious the ambulance has arrived. Morris opens the front door and lets the two paramedics in.

They have a stretcher and medical kit with them as they make their way to the small room where Dr. Bozivich is sitting in bed. She gets up and carries her little suitcase to leave but is told by one of the paramedics to remain seated because they needed to ask some questions and perhaps complete some paperwork before they leave.

One of the men starts to take details of her ailment; name, age etc. He asks her what her relationship with Morris was; she tells them he is her son. The men gaze at Morris in apparent disbelief, perhaps it is due to the fact that Morris is African and Dr. Bozivich is Russian.

However, one of the men starts to prepare the stretcher with which to take Dr. Bozivich to the ambulance, but she blatantly refuses, saying that she is not going to be carried on a stretcher. They all leave the house to the ambulance. Morris insists that he would come in the ambulance too to look after Dr. Bozivich but is assured by the paramedics that it isn't necessary for him to come along with them.

Although it is well past midnight when the ambulance finally leaves, the twitchings of her neighbours' curtains are noticed.

Morris is deep in thought as to what could be wrong with Dr. Bozivich that she would not tell him. Why did she give those paintings to him and showed him the picture of her daughter? There could be some hidden agenda; only time will reveal all the answers.

Chapter 16

The following day, Morris goes shopping. He picks up some varied fruits, a large box of chocolates and energy drinks, and hurries to the hospital where he enquires at reception for the location of Dr. Bozivich. He is directed to a ward upstairs, so he enters the lift and appears at the nurses' station, where some nurses are gathered. They show him Dr. Bozivich's bed.

Morris approaches the bedside, only to find her asleep or rather her eyes are closed. He sits down and starts to place his shopping on her bedside cabinet. Just at that moment Dr. Bozivich opens her eyes and smiles. Morris asks her if she was getting better, to which she answers with a nod indicating that she is feeling better. Morris asks many questions in order to initiate a conversation, but to no avail; rather she resorts to indicating with a nod in answer to his questions but does not say a single word.

Morris spends around forty minutes at her bedside then decides to leave. He goes back to the nurses and enquires about her. The nurses' response is that Dr. Bozivich constantly refuses to accept any food or drink and has not spoken to anyone since she was admitted. They also inform Morris that the doctor did not find anything wrong with her. They ask him if he was her next of kin, to which he does not answer but informs them that her daughter lives in Australia.

He gives them a box of chocolates and leaves.

Every day Morris visits Dr. Bozivich at the hospital; each time he buys fruits, flowers and some magazines for her but whenever he visits he finds the previous stock untouched, yet he still keeps on buying in the hope that one day she will consume them.

On the second week, he returns from visiting Dr. Bozivich and decides to telephone her daughter Amanda, and to tell her that her mother is in the hospital and will need her attention. However, when he called Amanda, she dropped the phone on him. She did not want to know in the slightest about her mother's condition or her circumstances. The time difference between Australia and London is substantial and he decides to wait until it is convenient for Amanda – then he would ring her again?

Chapter 17

Some weeks have gone by but Morris does not know the whereabouts of Isabbul or Kevin the tramp, and then, one Saturday night, Morris is relaxing with Henrietta in his lounge watching television when suddenly, she flicks the remote on to another programme. To their astonishment, Isabbul is on the programme being interviewed by a well-known journalist about his latest single that has topped the charts. Henrietta does not believe what she is witnessing, as for Morris, he is happily indifferent.

Journalist asks Isabbul on the TV, "You are a very young man who has never been heard of before. How did it all start?"

"It all started at the doorway of a supermarket". Replies Isabbul.

"The doorway of a supermarket?" Asks Journalist.

"Yeah". Replies Isabbul, "I was begging for money to get something to eat and this man enters... and my entire life changed from then on. He is an amazing human being and he taught me a lot about life".

"How did he change your life?" Asks Journalist.

"He influenced the way I think and elucidates what makes people suffer and what sets one free. In fact, he is what you might call a modern-day Buddha; completely selfless and much more concerned about the welfare and happiness of others. I can assure you he is the one who changed my destiny".

Isabbul focuses on the camera and says, "Morris if you are watching, thank you for all you have done for me, there is no single moment that passes that you are not in my thoughts, filled with gratitude for meeting you on that day."

He then turns, facing the journalist.

"Morris held a grand party in his house and invited me". He adds, "There, I met a lot of wonderful and beautiful people." He pauses. "That party was for me on my birthday; Morris gave me a brand new guitar as my birthday present."

At this point, tears of joy start rolling down Isabbul's cheeks.

"So I played a few songs and one of his friends at the party discovered me and my destiny positively changed, the rest is history."

Morris gazes at Henrietta in silent admiration and says.

"This is a typical example of when an iron is heated it makes a fine sword. He suffered a lot, that's why he is able to appreciate a positive change in his life. He made a cause for these changes and I am only an instrument to that effect. I am very happy for him that he has finally realised his dreams."

Henrietta remains speechless and she suddenly turns to Morris and says,

"He described you as a modern-day Buddha, what do you think he meant by that"?

Morris replies, "A Buddha is someone who is enlightened and Buddhism is a teaching of enlightenment and a

"Buddhist" is one who is striving to be enlightened through the practice of Buddhism.

The Buddha is absolutely free from suffering, he has achieved absolute happiness, that is, he or she is happy, irrespective of his or her circumstances. He relieves others of suffering and instils happiness and hope by teaching them how to do that. The Buddha won't do that for you but will teach you how to do it then it is up to the individual to follow the path and achieve it by himself or herself. When one is able to do that, one becomes a Buddha. In other words, everyone has the potential of becoming a Buddha".

Henrietta then asks, "Why does one need to make the sound of the sun in order to become a Buddha?"

Morris replies, "Liken an individual life to a car battery. If the battery is inactive, it cannot start a car, but the same battery when charged up, will be able to start a car; activate all the functions in the car – such as lights, heater, radio, air condition and other accessories within the car. It is the same battery which enables all these functions, the only difference is that it has been charged up."

"In the same way," he continues, "when one chants the sound of the sun, it positively transforms the individual's life and it draws out the individual's limitless potential. In the same way that a room which has been dark for years can be lit up with a single candlelight, or a grass lawn that is withering can be resuscitated by watering it. Therefore, when one chants the sound of the sun, all the good fortune which has been within one from timeless beginning, the innate wisdom, life force and true compassion, well up from within the individual's life. Through chanting the sound of the sun, the individual is constantly fusing his or her life with that of the universal law and he or she gains protection and is also able to see the true reality of all things, all one's good fortune is restored. These are some of the functions of the Mystic Law. It is the essence of good karma which transforms or changes the individual's poisons into medicine as you take actions in your daily life. One does not need to escape realities of life by going to the mountains, burying one's head in the sand or in isolation, but by taking actions amid the realities of life, transforming every situation to work positively for your benefit; this is the process of changing poison into medicine, it is the essence of true freedom and happiness."

Henrietta's face is beaming with joy just by listening to Morris's sincere explanations of his belief. She wonders why he is always ready and willing to explain in detail whenever he is asked a question about Buddhism.

"Do you fancy dinner at the village restaurant this evening?" Asks Morris.

"That will be nice but I have to go to my flat first to pay my rent to the landlord and will be ready about 9pm?" Replies Henrietta.

"Excellent, 9pm is fine. I have to go to the hospital to visit Dr. Bozivich and should be back by then". Says Morris.

"The eccentric elderly lady?" Asks Henrietta.

"Yes" Morris replies, "she has been refusing to eat or drink anything since she was admitted and the nurses have told me that the doctor did not find anything wrong with her health."

"She may be contemplating a kind of suicide" says Henrietta, "My great-grandmother died that way. She checked herself into a hospital and the doctor confirmed there was nothing wrong with her health – she refused to eat or drink for a few days and eventually passed away in the hospital through starvation".

Morris drops Henrietta off at her flat, goes shopping and purchases some grapes and bottles of energy drinks before going to the hospital. When he gets there, Dr. Bozivich's bed is empty, so he enquires from the nurses about her where-about. The nurses ask him to wait in the waiting room which is at the end of the ward. So, he goes to the waiting room and waits for about twenty minutes when a nurse comes to him and tells him that Dr. Bozivich had passed away about an hour or so before his arrival to the hospital.

He enquires where her body was and is told that it is in the small room adjacent to the nurses' station. He asks if it was possible for him to see the body. One of the nurses leads him to the room and opens the door. Morris also asks if he could be with Dr. Bozivich alone and the nurses agree and close the door and walk away, leaving Morris inside.

The body of Dr. Bozivich is laid out on a single bed. She is covered from her shoulders down to her feet. Her neck and head are the only parts of her body which remains uncovered. Morris gently walks round the bed in deep thought, he remembers their relationship since meeting her while cleaning out his car in the street corner, to dropping her off at the airport, to meeting Henrietta and so on. He then clasps his palms together and chants the sound of the sun, followed by a deep prayer for her eternal peace and happiness.

After that, he opens the door and walks back to the nurses' station where some nurses assemble and he gives them all his shopping that was meant for the late

Dr. Bozivich. He asks them to share the shopping or give it to the patients in the ward. A nurse asks if he knows of any next of kin of the late Dr. Bozivich, to which he replies that her daughter, Amanda, lives in Australia and promises to call her that evening and let her know that her mother has passed away this time. The nurses sympathise with him and thanked him for the shopping he leaves with them.

Morris hurries home and immediately calls Amanda. To Morris's surprise, Amanda picks up the phone and asks Morris, "Mother has died, hasn't she?"

Morris replies, "Yes, she passed away about two hours ago."

"Okay, I will be in London in a couple of days," says Amanda.

This time it is Morris who drops the phone in a shocking wonder. He does not understand why Amanda is very keen to come over to London in a couple of days' time, when her mother had passed away but would not come to see her when she was alive.

Around 9pm, Henrietta arrives at Morris's house dressed elegantly for their dinner date, but when Morris opens the door to her, she notices that he is not in good spirits contrary to his usual light-spirited attitude. This sets off an alarm bell that something is seriously wrong.

On entering, Henrietta holds Morris in a very tight embrace and asks him what was wrong. Morris replies that Dr. Bozivich had passed away that evening. The reality is that Morris is not too sad that she passed away because death is imperative to the living; he is rather sad about Amanda's attitude to the news of her mother's demise.

Morris and Henrietta walk over to Dr. Bozivich's house. As they enter, Henrietta is taken aback by the gothic nature of the furnishings and she starts to explore, room by room. Morris is collecting some of her mail for eventual notification of her demise to the senders. Then there is a scream from Henrietta; as she enters one of the rooms, she comes face-to-face with a framed picture of her mother hanging on the wall. Morris darts into the room where Henrietta screamed and sees Henrietta standing terrified as she faces the wall, starring at the picture of her mother. Morris, in silent wonder is watching her as she fixes her eyes on the picture.

Pointedly she says to Morris, "This is my mother!" Morris's jaw drops.

"If this is the picture of your mother, it is likely that Dr. Bozivich could have been your nan whom you have been searching for all this time," says Morris.

"Ironically, the first person that I spoke with on my arrival at the airport," replies Henrietta.

They start rummaging through the house in search of more clues. Henrietta opens a drawer to find an old envelope marked with Australian stamp. She opens the envelope and reads the letter inside it. It is from her mother, her mother's name and address are clearly written on it as the sender. Now that the jigsaw is almost complete, they immediately make their way swiftly to the hospital. Henrietta wants to take a good look at her nan, even though she is now dead.

They arrive at the hospital but she suddenly changes her mind and decides to come back at a later date, so they go back to Morris's house and order a take-away meal instead. There is no appetite to eat out as planned. Morris then asks Henrietta if her mother's name was Amanda. "How did you know that?" She asks.

Morris produces the telephone number given to him by Dr. Bozivich, that belonged to her daughter and also the address; the final jigsaw is now complete.

"This means that I have even telephoned your mother tonight to inform her that her mother is deceased," says Morris.

"And what did she say?" Henrietta asks anxiously.

Morris then tells her that Amanda will be coming over to the UK in a couple of days' time.

"Did you tell her that nan was ill and in the hospital?"

"Yes, I did, but when I phoned her this evening she seemed to know already that your nan had passed away – incredible! On the previous occasions when your nan was still alive Amanda would not speak to me, but constantly hung up on me."

The following morning, Morris and Henrietta are settled for breakfast when the doorbell rings. Henrietta opens the door to find Anthony and Kevin standing outside. Kevin is wearing a designer three piece suit. Anthony enters with Kevin following behind. Morris is surprised to see both of them together at his house early in the morning.

Morris asks Anthony, "What brought you guys to my house at this time in the morning?"

"To give you the good news, about Isabbul." Replies Anthony.

"What about him?" Asks Morris.

"He is now a big star. I saw him on the television being interviewed and he mentioned you were the key to his success." Replies Anthony.

"Yes, we also saw the programme". Says Morris, he turns to Kevin and says, "I hardly recognise you in that suit - how come?"

"Thank you Morris. It is a long way from being a tramp who used to live in the car park at St. Pancreas International". Replies Kevin.

"How is your dog?" Asks Morris.

"He is alright and we no longer fight for sausages". Replies Kevin.

"Kevin called me yesterday and asked me to bring him to your house to let you know their lives have changed, so here we are". Says Anthony.

Kevin says to Morris, "My life changed for the better after your party, that was when I met Isabbul and now I am his road manager. We have toured the whole of the US and Australia, and will have a gig at the O2 Arena soon. It was a dramatic change to our lives".

"Glad to hear", says Morris, "How is Isabbul, He definitely made an impression with his music at the party; they are still talking about him and his guitar-playing".

"He talked about coming to see you, so, expect him soon." Replies Kevin.

Henrietta, who had been quietly sitting aside and listening intently, begins pacing up and down the lounge and suddenly starts crying.

Anthony walks over to her, holds her hand and asks Morris,

"What is the matter with her?"

"You should ask her". Replies Morris.

Henrietta sobs as she explains, "It is so amazing that the lives of people who come in contact with Morris have profoundly changed for the better. I remember how he came into the supermarket car part with this young man who he did not know from Adam and they both went for a meal and next thing, he invites him to a party held for his birthday and now this young man has realised his dream"

"I take it she is referring to Isabbul" says Anthony.

"Yes", says Morris.

Henrietta continues. "And as for Kevin, we met him in St. Pancreas International car park fighting with his dog and now his life has changed beyond recognition. Morris has also had positive effect on my own life; the effect is immeasurable."

"Have I told you guys that Henrietta and I are engaged to be married and that all of you are invited to the wedding?" Asks Morris.

"Can I be of use at the wedding, I mean, I want to help". Persists Kevin.

"I am sure you will be of great help, we will find you something to do - thank you for the thought". Replies Morris.

"When is the wedding?" Asks Anthony.

"After the funeral". Replies Morris.

"Whose funeral?" Anthony asks.

"My nan's, she passed away yesterday. Replies Henrietta.

Anthony knew that Henrietta is from Australia and perhaps he assumes that her nan was in Australia when she died:

"Does it mean you will be going to Australia for the funeral?" Anthony asks".

"No, her house is just around the corner. She was my neighbour" Replies Morris.

Anthony looks puzzled, and says to Morris, "You never tell me anything - Morris, why did I not know that Henrietta's nan was your neighbour?"

Morris is hesitant for a while and then says to Anthony, "I did not know neither did Henrietta that her nan lived in the UK let alone she'd been my neighbour", he pauses "Never mind...it's a long story - Anthony."

Morris and Kevin leave.

Henrietta decides to go back to her flat and call her mother. Morris is driving her to her flat and tells her that it is not necessary to call Amanda as she could already be on her way to the UK. He drops Henrietta off and returns to his house.

Chapter 18

Three days later

Amanda arrives in London from Australia and calls
Morris to let him know that she is in town. She also asks
him to get the keys to her mother's house as she does not
have any keys and cannot get in. Morris asks Amanda
where she was and she replies that she is standing in
front of her mother's house. Morris hurries over with
the keys.

When he gets near to the house, he sees Amanda
from a distance pacing to and fro. He recognises her
from the picture but as Amanda had not seen him before,
she hasn't the faintest idea of who to expect. Morris
approaches her and introduces himself and goes straight
to the front door and opens it. Amanda goes in with her
little suitcase and instantly starts to remove the paintings
from the wall. Morris is dumbfounded and asks Amanda
if she wants something to eat but she replies that she
had eaten on the plane and is not hungry. He did not tell
Amanda about her daughter, Henrietta. Amanda has no
knowledge of her whereabouts since she left Australia
about two years earlier.

Morris leaves Amanda in the house and goes to get a
key cut. He returns a few minutes later and hands over
the duplicate, and gives her details of the hospital where

her mother's body is at rest, which is only a couple of miles away.

Morris then returns to his house and starts to pray for the eternal peace and happiness of Dr. Bozivich.

Four days later, Henrietta calls Morris on the phone to enquire if her mother had arrived. He tells her that she arrived six days ago, that he had let her into Dr. Bozivich's house.

Henrietta had been to the hospital alone to see her nan's body twice and had been purchasing some clothes in which her nan would be buried. She had also informed the hospital that her mother would be arriving in the UK from Australia for the funeral.

Henrietta wonders if her mother has been to the hospital to see her nan's body. She takes a cab and arrives at Morris's house and they both go over to Dr. Bozivich's house. When Morris enters, Amanda is busy ripping off the carpets from the floorboards; she hasn't noticed that Henrietta is following behind Morris and at that moment, Amanda lifts her head and sees Henrietta; she is in an instant state of shock and bewilderment. Amanda stands up erect and her face turns blue and red at the same time as if she has seen a ghost. Henrietta leans by the entrance behind the door gazing at her mother with disgust.

Morris asks Amanda if she had been to the hospital to see her mother's body. Amanda replies that she had not.

Henrietta says, "It has been six days since you arrived and you haven't spared the time to go and see nan at the hospital, but you have the time to rip the carpets up from the floorboards – what is the matter with you?"

"Why did you not tell me that you have been staying with her all this time?" Replies Amanda.

"I have not", replies Henrietta furiously, "I did not even know she was here, neither did I know she was my nan who I have been looking for all this time. I came in here with Morris after she passed away to find your picture hanging on the wall in the living room. So, I put two and two together to solve the mystery that she was my nan."

"Why are you ripping the carpet off and taking the paintings down from the wall?" Morris asks.

Not waiting for a reply, he walks passed Amanda into the kitchen and looks into the garden to find different kinds of furniture, crockery, and various antiques assembled together in heaps as if they were waiting to be collected.

Apparently Amanda had been in the loft and in some rooms and got all the stuff together to sell.

Morris leaves Henrietta and Amanda and goes back to his house. As he turns a corner leading to his house he notices a courier ringing his doorbell, so he increases his stride and meets the courier at his door.

"What have you got for me?" Morris asks.

The courier hands over a clipboard and says, "Sign here."

Morris signs and the courier gives him a package. He takes it and enters his house. When he opens the package it contains two special tickets to the O2 for Isabbul's concert, for him and Henrietta. These tickets include being picked up in a limousine to and from the concert, and front row sitting. Inside the package there is also a small handwritten note by Isabbul which reads:

"Hello Morris. Please accept this invitation. It will make me very happy indeed to see you and Henrietta at the gig. Remember you caused all this and you have completely changed my life for the best." Signed: *Isabbul.*

A few minutes later, Henrietta turns up., Morris shows her the concert tickets and the note from Isabbul. She reads the note and thoughtfully gazes at Morris.

"We have to go Morris, what do you think"?

"Yeah, we have to go," he confirms.

"Has Amanda made any arrangements for your nan's funeral?" asks Morris.

"She has not even seen the body yet, and you talk about funeral". Replies Henrietta.

"Did she tell you when she will be going to the hospital?" Asks Morris.

"Not at all, she was still immensely astonished to see me at Nan's house". Says Henrietta.

"I bet she was. Never in a million years would she have expected that'.

Says Morris.

Since the date of the funeral has not been set, Henrietta suggests that whatever happens, they have to attend the concert at the 02, in a couple of weeks. If the date of the funeral clashes with the date of the concert, the funeral's date would have to be postponed or brought forward.

⁂

On the eight day since Amanda arrived, Morris and Henrietta go over to Dr. Bozivich's house to find out what preparations Amanda has accomplished.

To their disappointment, she has not been to the hospital to see her mother's body, despite the fact that it has been eight days since her arrival and the hospital is only a couple miles away.

Henrietta is disgusted and angry about her mother's heartless behaviour, coupled with the fact that all the furniture in the house has been sold, including the rugs and carpets. The house is completely empty. Henrietta and her mother Amanda are engaged in a very serious exchange of words which develops into an intensive argument. Morris tries to be a mediator but to no avail, he is unable to make them stop the argument so he leaves and goes back to his house. Henrietta returns to Morris's house after confrontation with Amanda.

Morris says to Henrietta, "I think it is only right that you move in with me since we will be getting married after your nan's funeral."

"If only my nan would have been alive to witness my big day," replies Henrietta with a concoction of deep regret and joy.

"As you do not have a lot of things to carry, I will use the car to bring all your belongings," continues Morris.

Henrietta approaches him and gives him a big prolonged and determined hug.

Morris and Henrietta did not go back to Dr. Bozivich's house for two weeks and Amanda did not contact them to confirm when the funeral will take place.

Morris does not want to interfere with the family arrangements since he is only an outsider, despite the fact that he looked after Dr. Bozivich in her last months. His decision not to intrude was strong but not easy. So, at the end of the second week after Henrietta moved in with Morris, they decided to visit the hospital in order to find out if any arrangements were being made for Dr. Bozivich's funeral. To their surprise, they were told by the nurses that Amanda had only popped in that day for the first time, which means that since she arrived in the UK over three weeks ago she had only visited the hospital ones.

Morris and Henrietta therefore, left the hospital and drove directly to Dr. Bozivich's house to contact Amanda; this will inevitably give Henrietta an opportunity to confront her mother again.

Most unexpectedly, on reaching Dr. Bozivich's house they notice a man clutching a clipboard and an electronic measuring device, walking round the house, taking measurements of the property and entering the record on his clipboard. Henrietta gets out of the car, approaches the man and enquires what he was doing. He replies that he is recording details of the house because he has been instructed to put the house in an auction for sale. Henrietta furiously snatches the clipboard from him and storms into the now empty house to confront her mother.

Morris, aware of the impending row between Henrietta and Amanda, is sitting comfortably in his car. He does not want to interfere in a row between mother and daughter; obviously there is no doubt about which side he is on – Henrietta's of course. Nevertheless, he thinks that it is better to leave them alone to sort it all out by themselves.

The man who received instructions to sell the house is in total astonishment, he goes to the car to speak to Morris.

He is trembling with fright as he asks Morris, "Can you tell me what is going on?"

"You should ask them, I do not wish to get involved in a row between mother and daughter," replies Morris.

"So, this young lady is the daughter of the woman whom I received instruction from?"

"Yes, and this property belonged to her grandmother. Do not worry, I am sure it will be sorted in their own time," replies Morris.

A few minutes later, Henrietta emerges from the house, enters the car and slams the car door angrily. Morris drives off back to his house.

When they are settled in the house, there is a long silence, none of them is talking. Eventually, Henrietta asks Morris if they could arrange for her nan's funeral because she did not think her mother has any intention of doing anything about it. Morris is thoughtful for a while and feels that it makes sense that he organised the funeral because considering Amanda's attitude to the whole affair, she may not be interested in giving her a reasonable funeral.

So, Morris starts ringing the funeral directors, council offices and any institution that may be connected with finalising arrangements for a funeral.

Within minutes, he has completed the whole procedure and he starts off by sending off some cheques accordingly. He then gives three dates to Henrietta to choose from, for her nan's funeral.

Chapter 19

The funeral

On the day of the funeral, Morris is in the car with Henrietta stationed in front of Dr. Bozivich's house, while Amanda is in another car also stationed in front of Dr. Bozivich's house; all waiting for the coffin to be brought by the funeral directors so that Dr Bozivich's body will be rested in front of her house for a while before the onward procession to the cemetery.

Shortly before noon, a couple of hearses are seen proceeding to the house; most of the neighbours come out to pay their last respects. The hearse which is carrying the coffin goes directly to the front of the house and stops. There is silence for some minutes before Henrietta and Morris walk up to the driver of the hearse, Amanda follows. They have a little chat together and the procession starts to the cemetery. The entire procession comprises of two cars and two hearses. One of the cars is Morris's.

The cemetery is about four miles from Dr. Bozivich's house. When they get to the cemetery, everyone is seated while the coffin is made ready for cremation.

Morris makes an emotional speech; he speaks not only of Dr. Bozivich's virtues but also some of her vices, which could be said to be common to almost everybody.

A musician, who Morris hired for the occasion, plays an acoustic guitar and sings a farewell song; after which, the coffin was cremated.

After the ceremony, Morris invites Amanda to his house for a drink and something to eat, to which Amanda reluctantly accepts, although she does not get on well with her daughter.

It is around 2pm when they reach Morris's house. He orders a Thai take-away meal, which they devour without hesitation.

Amanda asks Morris how he met her mother. Morris replies that it was in the street when he was cleaning out his car; he also explains a few circumstances of their relationship in brief.

Morris does not ask her about the rift between her and her mother, neither does Henrietta speak to her mother. After what seems to be the best part of two hours, Amanda leaves and promises to let Morris know of her arrangements before going back to Australia.

Little does Morris and Henrietta know that it is the last time they will ever see Amanda again, for no sooner than the house is sold in an auction, Amanda transfers the whole money from the sale of Dr. Bozivich's house to Australia and she leaves for Australia with all the remuneration from the sale of the contents too.

Henrietta tries many times to reach her on the phone but to no avail, she was not picking up the phone. Morris tried to console her but Henrietta could not let go. She wrote several letters to her but the letters were returned to sender.

Some weeks later, she contacted the auctioneers who sold the house to enquire if they were in contact with her mother, but they confirmed that they had no further transactions with her therefore they had no reason to contact her anymore. However, Henrietta was referred to the solicitor who did the conveyance. She contacted the solicitor who said that Amanda had informed her that she had also sold her house in Western Australia and bought another house near Sydney, and that was all she knew and no more.

Henrietta was disillusioned and frustrated and gave up looking for Amanda.

Chapter 20

Isabbul's gig

The following weekend is to be the date for Isabbul's gig at the O2 Arena, so, Henrietta and Morris start getting ready for it.

In the evening of that day, they are picked up by a chauffeur-driven limousine and taken to the O2 Arena's special entrance area, where two security officers welcome them and lead them to the front row just in front of the stage. The O2 Arena is full and many fans are holding placards up which read: *The one and only Isabbul.*

A waitress arrives with a bottle of well-chilled champagne and special popcorn and begins to serve Henrietta and Morris. All this is with the compliments of Isabbul. The band is settled after tuning the guitars and so on, except for the front man, Isabbul, who is not in sight at that moment. Suddenly he appears, clutching the very guitar that Morris gave him on his birthday. He walks over to the front of the stage, grabs the microphone and looks in the direction where Morris and Henrietta are sitting and says, "Tonight is particularly a special night and a special gig for me. Why? Because he caused this event to happen, without him, there would be no Isabbul and there would be no music and equally none of you would be here tonight. My life changed dramatically when I came into contact with this extraordinary human being and since then the rest has been history."

The crowd are so silent that one could hear a pin drop. Everyone is in anticipation wondering who this person might be.

Isabbul continues, "I used to live in the streets, begging for some cash to buy some food and my residence at the time was under Waterloo Bridge. The rest of the story is on my website so please visit it and discover the magic that triggered a positive and dramatic change in my life; the magic that is responsible for this concert. Ladies and gentlemen, please put your hands together for Morris!"

Isabbul goes to where Morris is sitting, holds him by the hand and leads him to the stage. The crowd are hysterical with excitement and give both men a standing ovation.

Morris bows and says, "Everything is possible when one embraces the "way of the sun"," and he goes back to his seat.

Isabbul then starts to sing and play his guitar. He starts off singing the same song that he played at his birthday party; *Wonderful Tonight*, as a special dedication to Morris and Henrietta.

During the interval, Kevin joins Morris and Henrietta. It is undoubtedly quite a memorable occasion for all of them. At the end of the concert Morris and Henrietta are led to the Limousine by the same two security officers. When they enter they are met by Isabbul and Kevin, who are already seated in the same Limousine.

"That was quite a gig, Isabbul". Morris remarks.

"Thank you. It is really a pleasure to see you. Kevin told me you will be getting married to Henrietta soon". Says Isabbul.

"Yes". Replies Morris.

Henrietta happily chuckles and says "How news travel so fast".

"Can I play on your wedding day?" Asks Isabbul with pleasure.

"I will be delighted." Morris replies.

"Really?" Says Henrietta.

"It will be my pleasure to honour you in that way. Can I personally arrange for the reception to be here – at the O2 Arena?" Asks Isabbul

"Morris who always prefers low key events quickly declines the offer and says to Isabbul "I want none of that, the reception will be at my place, in my garden. Thank you for your kind thought anyway."

"For some reason, I knew Morris won't want that, he is just not that sort of person". Says Henrietta.

"We are on the same wave length", Kevin says to Henrietta "Morris is just not that sort of person."

"You used to say some profound and philosophical things to me Morris, and I have always lived by them, have you got any advice for me tonight? Asks Isabbul.

"I am glad you asked. Number One is do not be swayed by any of the eight winds". Says Morris.

"Eight winds?" Asks Isabbul.

"Yes, Morris replies, "it is Buddhist concept and there are eight of them, and one of the eight says – "do not be swayed by either success or failure".

I am going to pass on more wisdom to you and they are not connected with the eight winds but they are very essential.

Morris starts writing them down on a piece of paper:

"Today I rededicate my life to everyone's happiness;
To be strong so that nothing can upset my peace of
mind;
To talk health, happiness and hope to every person
I meet;
To make friends feel there is something good and
beautiful in them;
To look at the sunny side of everyting and to be
optimistic about life;
To think only the best, work towards doing and
expecting only the best.
To be just as happy about the success of others as I am
about the success of myself;
To forget any mistakes of the past and press forward
to greater achievement in the future;
To give so much time to improving myself that I have
no time to criticise others;
To be too strong for fear, too kind for anger and too
happy to worry;
To lift my heart in faith each day so that the Mystic
Law may show in my life."

When he has written it down, he passes it over to Isabbul and says, "This is the diary of a very wise man, my mentor. He is called sensei which means "teacher". His real name is Daisaku Ikeda. If you live by these every day, and make the sound of the sun, there is nothing to fear – absolutely nothing."

Isabbul accepts the piece of paper with deep appreciation and he and Kevin leave the limo. The chauffeur drives Morris and Henrietta home.

Chapter 21

A few days after the concert, Isabbul's website is flooded with traffic as his fans are very inquisitive to read the whole story about how Morris, who is African, could have influenced Isabbul's transition of destiny to stardom.

Their curiosity as evident on a few websites, stems from the fact that Morris is African, and he is not really a professional musician, therefore, what could have brought them together in the first place, and motivated him to help Isabbul as much as he did?

The main point is that Morris said something on the stage that "Everything is possible when one embraces the way of the sun". That sentence, though profound but ultimately beyond their comprehension, they wish to find out more about; with the view that whatever it means, if it could work for Isabbul they need some of that too.

By sheer coincidence or a mere connection in life's tapestry, James and his girlfriend, Mona, attended the concert at the O2 and recognised Morris when Isabbul took him to the stage. They are the couple who were in the small crowd within the St. Pancreas car park and witnessed Kevin beating up his dog for the sake of a sausage. They saw clearly that Morris was the same person who intervened, the same person who gave Kevin ten pounds with which to buy some sausages for himself and for his dog, while a small crowd, including themselves, just stood by and watched. As a result, James and Mona put something about that incident on their website and that attracted a lot of hits as well.

Anthony calls Morris to inform him what he has read on his friend's website. It is to do with their anxiety of knowing why Morris went out of his way to help Isabbul to achieve mega-stardom when they are neither the same colour nor the same race or even friends.

Morris replies, "Some people may argue that tribalism is not acceptable in any form. Religion, colour and race breed tribalism. However, certain religions can be exempt so long as it aspires towards equality and the common good."

You belong to one tribe, it builds a wall against the others who do not belong to the same tribe as you – it causes exclusion.

On the contrary, through enlightenment we undoubtedly realise there are no tribes, we can positively accommodate all people, we can also understand that all life is the same. Our lives and the life of the universe are the same, hence there is no "self" – the only difference is the mind. Through aspiring for enlightenment one can cultivate a pure mind, and also purifies the other senses, and one can realise that all lives are worthy of respect. You can see that tribalism is just sheer ignorance. Enlightenment causes inclusiveness of all peoples."

Anthony is intently listening with apparent admiration of the wisdom in the speech. When Morris had finished, he asks Morris to repeat the whole thing again – this time, Anthony is writing it down with the intention of putting it on to his website.

"He says to Morris, "Have you ever been in any difficulty in your life so far?"

Morris replies, "Good question, the answer is "Yes, and many times too."

Anthony asks, "Could you tell me one of those difficulties?" Morris starts to explain. "Without overcoming difficulties one would not know happiness; difficulties or obstacles enable one to transform oneself from within. In dealing with difficulties, one strengthens one's life and is ready to deal with the next one. It is an opportunity for one to grow as long as one faces it head on. There is no end to learning, neither is there an end to encountering difficulties. It is rather an illusion to think otherwise. Happiness is therefore an ability to overcome them whenever they emerge because they will always certainly emerge."

He continues, "I was lying in bed one spring morning around 3am, my telephone was ringing persistently, when I picked it up it was my sister on the other end of the line – by the way it was an international call. The news was that my dear mother had passed away. I instantly descended into an incredible abyss of irreconcilable loss and I started playing back in my mind the last time that I went to see her and stayed with her for a week in her hospital bed. It soon dawned on me then that I would never see her again.

Three months earlier, I had received a call from my sister that my mother was admitted in the hospital and that she might not make it. That necessitated my booking a flight immediately and I went to Africa to be with her, as perhaps it could be her last days and probably the last time I would see her alive. At that time she was approaching one hundred years old.

When I got to the airport in Africa, my brother was waiting to take me home in his car to get changed, have a meal and then we would go to the hospital to see our mother. Contrary to his plans, I asked him to take me directly to the hospital. When we got there she was sitting up in bed and a doctor was examining her for further treatment. As soon as I walked in she saw me, and at that moment it seemed her illness had completely disappeared, for as soon as I approached her bedside, she grabbed me intensely and hugged me and would not let go. The doctor stood bemused for a while and left the room.

When she finally let go of me, I sat on the bed and we began to chat. I took out a comb from her bedside cabinet and started combing her hair gently. She was smiling with delight and soon we were both laughing together joyfully. I stayed with her at the hospital without going home to our family house. I changed my clothes there and had bathed there.

My mother was staying in a private ward, a self-contained room, with her own shower facility, toilet and a television. At night, I would sleep on the floor. My brother would go home and prepare some food with our house-maids, as my dear mother would not accept hospital food or any type of food prepared by someone outside of the family. It was not because of distrust but because, simply she maintained pure hygiene even in her old age. She was always conscious of the hygiene of what she ate or drank."

Anthony who is all ears then asks, "What happened next?"

Morris continues, "After a couple of weeks, the doctor said she was ready to go home and gave me the list of various medicines that she would be taking at home. I was so happy that I called all the nurses that looked after her and thanked them from the bottom of my heart and offered them some small amount of cash. The doctor later on remarked that my dear mother got better suddenly as soon as she saw me. After all that, I gladly took her home and looked after her with my sister until my return to the UK. It seems that this time around it was not meant to be."

"So your sister called to say your mother has passed". Anthony asks.

"Yes". Replies Morris.

"And all the memories of last time came flooding back. Inevitably, I had to go to Africa again, but this time for the funeral. My dear mother had the highest title amongst the women, the only woman ever to hold the title of "Erico", it is a very rare title and it is recognised and respected far and wide. She helped a lot of people and settled quarrels between husband and wife, father and son, mother and daughter and so on. As a mark of respect, everyone in the village gathered in our house and stayed for ten days till after the funeral. The number was approximately five thousand people, we have a large compound. There were also relatives and well-wishers from Europe, UK, and the USA.; My sister booked accommodation for them which we paid for, in the nearby hotels. Village chiefs from the neighbouring towns also gathered to pay their respects, including variety of traditional dance groups. We would had to feed everyone. This is the tradition in some African countries particularly if the deceased was from a certain kind of family or was distinguished."

"For ten days?" Asks Anthony.

"Yes, night and day. As this would require a lot of cash, I cleared my bank account, and went to Africa.

Though my sister Played a major financial role. I spent a whole thirty days over there and on my return to the UK there were lots of letters that were piled up behind my front door, mostly bills, such as energy bills, water bills, insurance bills and telephone bills. These have accumulated as they usually come almost at the same time, and some of them had "late reminders" too, plus the mortgage payment which was overdue. There was no money to pay for any of that". Says Morris.

"My goodness! What a situation to be in, what did you do?" Asks Anthony.

Morris continues, "I took a decision that I needed a second job, any job as soon as possible, though I still had my proper full time job. As they say - desperate circumstances require desperate measures, also the Buddha said that 'great evil portends the arrival of great good'. As the universal law intended, my car documents such as insurance, MOT and road fund licence were still legal, which means they had not expired. So I got in my car and visited all the supermarkets and DIY stores and filled a lot of part-time job applications but received negative responses. I did not lose hope; after all, life without hope is not worth living. One day, after a very intensive search for a job to no avail, I was coming home a little dejected. As I looked across from a bridge, I noticed a large store which seemed to be busy at the time because the car park was full of cars so I decided to drive in and ask for a job. When I got in, I said to a man at the check-out that I would like to see the manager to which he replied, "I am the manager, how can I help you?"

I told him that I was looking for a job, any part-time job. He looked at me from head to toe and asked me for my telephone number and said he would ring me the following day for an interview. He telephoned me the following day and asked me to come over in the evening of that same day. When I turned up at the store he was informed by one of his staff that I was waiting by the front of the store. He came to me and invited me to follow him upstairs. We proceeded to what looked like a staff common room and sat down by a desk. He placed an application form in front of me and asked me to complete it. It was just a one page form which I completed in no time at all.

There and then, he asked me when I would like to start. I replied "tomorrow". He led me downstairs and introduced me to one of his assistant managers who included my name in the rota for the following day, and the rest is history. I prioritised the bills to be paid first and called all the companies that I needed to pay and settled with them. They agreed that I paid in instalments to clear the amount. It really took me a long time to completely pay everything off but I did pay them off. I remember those days; whenever there was a knock on my door I would not open just in case it was the people that I owed money to, and constantly thought that my electricity, gas or telephone would be disconnected at any time.

Believe me, it was a hard struggle at the time but it has strengthened my life. One learns a lot through experiencing difficulty, as the saying goes, that "experience is the best teacher' I have moved on since then".

Chapter 22

Morris, however, has become the main subject of discussion on websites and facebook. His reputation is growing like wild fire and everyone wants to know what the sound of the sun is all about.

Consequently, Morris has been invited to chat shows on the radio and television but he has declined all insisting that he does not find anything that he has done to be extraordinary. He maintains that everyone should be doing what they are supposed to do, "help each other". For every action there is equal and opposite reaction and that is even basic science.

Meanwhile, Isabbul has been touring the US, the Far East, Australia and Europe and each time he goes on the stage, he talks about Morris being responsible for turning his life around and for his positive change in good fortune, by simply meeting him.

As for Henrietta; she has now moved in to Morris's house and they are living together. One evening, they return from the Wimbledon village restaurant, Morris goes into the bathroom and Henrietta is relaxed on the sofa thinking about how her life has been so far. She reflects how she travelled most countries in search of her nan. How the whole incident of meeting an elderly lady at the airport connected her with Morris, how events have unfolded to reveal that the elderly lady,

Dr. Bozivich, was in fact her nan, but neither of them realised they were related. As a result of that meeting at the airport she is now living with Morris and about to be married to him; the man she adores and respects, the man she has been leaning on throughout her turbulence in the UK. She suddenly realises how her life has changed for the best beyond her wildest dream and tears begin to roll down her cheeks.

Nevertheless, her only regret was that she did not realise that Dr. Bozivich was her nan when she was alive.

Morris comes out of the bathroom to see Henrietta in a state; he is deeply concerned as he does not have a clue why she was crying. He joins her in the sofa and starts to wipe off the tears from her face. She holds him very tight and whispers in his ear:

"They are tears of joy, my life has turned three hundred and sixty degrees towards happiness since we met and I am very happy beyond belief that we are together."

It is a relief to Morris who joyfully replies, "Karma is the driver of this circumstance and indeed all circumstances, while cause and effect is the origin of karma and the sound of the sun is the basis for creating instant good karma. It destroys all bad karma and restores one's good fortune; I will do my best to protect and look after you. When one's karma changes, lives tapestry changes accordingly".

Henrietta asks emphatically, "So what is the sound of the sun?"

Morris looks directly into her eyes and says, "The sound of the sun is nothing other than NAM-MYO-HO-RENGE-KYO. It is the name of the universal law which is inherent in each one of us. It is not outside of ourselves. As one starts to chant this phrase one is calling the Buddha within and it will definitely emerge and one's life is instantly aligned with the universal rhythm. It is common knowledge that it is easier to swim with the tide than swim against it.

With excitement, Henrietta says, "I have read how this phrase changed someone's life very dramatically, she is a very famous musician, an American. I think it was also shown on TV".

"The law is non-discriminatory. It is in fact everyone's right and not a privilege; the wisdom, compassion and life force which are innate in the individual's life will emerge naturally without fail. The individual will begin to see the true nature that is the reality of all things". Morris adds.

"Great! Henrietta exclaims, "I am all for it. You are a fine example of the effects of this law"

"Thank you, but remember, you can fulfil your live, and live a life without regrets when you practice this Law". Says Morris.

Chapter 23

Wedding Day

It is mid-November in the UK, all the clocks have been set back one hour in the previous month, which means that one hour has been gained and the day is shorter than night.

The wedding will take place in a week's time. As in winter, the days are usually dark and cold, and the nights chilly and gloomy. There is frost in the mornings when all the car windscreens are covered with frost or ice. Henrietta is concerned about the weather on their forthcoming wedding and she never stops expressing her concern to Morris, but each time Morris is nonchalant to the overwhelming concerns aired by her and some of his friends about the expected bad weather on their wedding day. However, In the morning of the big day, Henrietta is being assisted by Sharon, Paris and Grace with make-up; they are the three cleaners who she had contracted to give Morris's house a good clean some time ago. They are all anxious about the weather because if it fails to turn out well before the afternoon, it will ruin the big occasion for them.

As tradition would have it, Morris should not be with the bride just before the wedding and because of that he is staying at Anthony's house to get ready.

The marriage Registry is about three miles from Morris's house. It is an old historic building which stands majestically almost in the middle of woodland surrounded by much matured trees in the distance. The ambiance radiates solemn serenity. A large car park is in the foreground.

Morris is accompanied by Anthony and arrives earlier at the Register Office. They notice that the car park is almost full but not a single person is in sight. The receptionist leads them into a room upstairs to wait for the bride and to confirm the entries in their marriage certificate before the ceremony.

The receptionist goes back to the reception, which is behind the building, to find a lot of people gathering at the back and starts to wonder why that is happening. He is busy with organising the wedding that is to take place and does not have the time to enquire why they are gradually filling up that area.

Very soon after that, Henrietta is on her way with Sharon and Grace in a comfortable car; Paris is driving. As they turn into the grounds of the Register Office, a crowd are seen heading the same way to the Register Office and none of them are among their guests, so they start to wonder. When Henrietta and her friends reach the main entrance, they are taken into one of the rooms to wait and also for Henrietta to complete and confirm the entries in the marriage certificate.

By this time the sky is brightening up and the sun begins to force itself through the clouds. Anthony peers through the upstairs window of the room in which they are waiting and yells "Morris look at that – the sun is coming through!"

Morris replies, "I have been expecting it to come through. I believe the sun will shine on my wedding day."

Morris and Anthony are led to the room downstairs where the marriage is to take place. Here, they join some of their guests who are already waiting but the bride is still in another room.

A few minutes later, the bride and her maids enter.

Henrietta is glowing in her ivory-coloured wedding dress; the tiara on her head sparkling and projecting spots of lights on the curtains and walls inside the room. The guests stand and applaud the beautiful bride on her dazzling entry to be unionised with Morris.

Henrietta wishes that moment never ends. Her desire is eventually about to be realised beyond her wildest dream. As the bride and the groom get seated facing the registrar for their declaration and vows, the sun fully emerges majestically through the clouds; its golden bright rays burst into the room jubilantly as if to indicate that the wedding is for eternal bliss or perhaps to bear witness at the union. Whatever the case may be - it is surely and joyfully witnessed by everyone. The weather in late November in the UK has never been known to display such a revitalising energy.

Call it coincidence or what you will, the fact is that the weather is pleasant on their wedding day and it is in November. It also stayed like that all day, contrary to everyone's expectation, except of course, for Morris.

As they step outside for photographs there is a gently breeze – so gentle that it does not beleaguer the branches on the trees.

Then suddenly, a large number of people from the back of the building; from all spectrums of life, begin to gather gradually around the bride and groom and begin to chant the sound of the sun in unison to glorify Morris and Henrietta's wedding.

Morris is inevitably surprised and overwhelmed since he had not told many people at that point how to make the sound of the sun; it must have leaked out somehow. Nevertheless, he is certainly pleased to hear that phrase, "NAM-MYO-HO-RENGE-KYO", which is the sound of the sun, being chanted by so many people.

Before the wedding, Isabbul and Kevin had made excuses that they had a very important recording to do and informed Morris and Henrietta that they would be unable to come to the Register Office, but would definitely make it to the reception at Morris's house.

As the sound of cameras click in the grounds of the Register Office, a motorcade of limousines and a couple of coaches arrive, with Isabbul and Kevin in a white limo in front leading the motorcade. There are cheers and applause from the crowd. Although Morris did not want it that way as he had planned his wedding to be low-key, he is certainly pleased that it has turned out like this.

The white limo pulls up beside Morris and Henrietta in the grounds of the Register Office. Isabbul and Kevin open the door of the white limo for Morris, Henrietta, Anthony and Parish and they enter, while some of the crowd and guests enter the other limos. The rest of the crowd enter the coaches. They drive off, all heading to Morris's house for the reception.

Chapter 24

Reception at Morris's House

The whole garden is decorated with balloons under the canopy that stretches its length and width. Gas-fired heaters are installed in every corner to provide heat. Chairs are placed around every table and caterers are ready to serve a sumptuous meal and a great variety of drinks stocked for the occasion. On the platform, which is erected as the stage, are a complete set of Isabbul's band's equipment. All of Morris's neighbours are there in a cheerful mood interacting with each other. Prior to this occasion, the neighbours did not have time for one another and had never been in conversation with one another. This has changed it all. They are introducing themselves to each other in friendly demeanour.

The arrival of the motorcade caused the neighbouring streets to be littered with limos. When all the guests disembark, they enter the garden in silent wonder as jaws drop due to the provisions and facilities which unfolds at the sight of them.

Morris turns to Isabbul.

"When was all these arranged?" Asks Morris.

"That was our reason for not coming to the Register Office on time". Says Isabbul.

"I suppose you invited my neighbours too". Asks Morris.

"We had to invite them so there will be no complaints about music being loud when the band plays". Replies Keven.

"Thanks to you both for all of this" says Morris.

"Do not mention it, nothing that we will ever do for you will surpass the words of wisdom and kindness you have lavishly given us". Says Isabbul.

"Most importantly is introducing us to the sound of the sun". Kevin adds.

"Morris - without you all of this would not have been possible", Says Isabbul, "It also reminds me of how my life started, in this very garden".

The reception lasts till the early hours of the following day, bringing all kinds of personalities in one place and uniting them as one in mind – to know and interact with one another in perfect harmony. It seems to be a great achievement for the neighbours who hardly spoke to one another previously.

❧ ❧

Two days later, Henrietta and Morris settle down with a cup of tea while opening their wedding presents.

Morris asks Henrietta. "Do you know what I will like to do?"

"Go on honeymoon"? Replies Henrietta.

"We will do that", but I think we should move to a different neighbourhood".

Henrietta is a little confused at Morris's suggestion especially as their neighbours are now interacting and talking to one another.

Henrietta suggests to Morris that it may not be wise to move now since their neighbours are now getting used to them and to one another since their wedding – unlike before.

Morris maintains that it is because of that reason that they should move, in order to catalyse another neighbourhood to do the same, In other words, to be friendly with one another. Henrietta is thoughtful for a while:

"That will be a mammoth task". She says, "Does it mean that we have to keep moving house in order to achieve that?"

"Not really", Replies Morris, "eventually it will have a domino effect; the law of cause and effect will get them to be like this one. Individual neighbours will start changing from within. It can change the whole community, towns and even countries, through the revolution of a single mind".

There is a knock on the front door and Henrietta opens the front door and finds three men in suits standing on the doorstep.

"Can I help you gentlemen?" Asks Henrietta.

One of the men starts to introduce himself and the other two.

"I am Barrister John Jones, and my colleagues are Mr Dickenson from the probate office and Mr Foster – may we come in?"

"Yes, please do come in". Says Henrietta.

She holds the door open for them and they enter. Morris stands up and introduces himself.

"Congratulations on your wedding". Says Barrister John Jones

Morris and Henrietta are surprised that he congratulates them for their wedding when they do not know who the three men were.

"Thank you". Replies Henrietta.

"How can we help you gentlemen?" Asks Morris.

"Madam," says Barrister John Jones to Henrietta, "it is about the 'will' of your grandmother, Dr. Bozivich, who passed away some months ago.

"Yes", what about her?" Asks Henrietta.

"Could you show us your passport or any form of original document bearing your name before we can go further", requests barrister John Jones, "Just to confirm we've got the right person".

Henrietta darts into the bedroom and retrieves her passport and birth certificate and gives them to Barrister John Jones. He goes through them meticulously and passes them to the other two gentlemen, who in turn read through them. They are now satisfied they have the right person.

Barrister John Jones hands over a large envelope to Henrietta "This is for you, there is a cheque and list of valuables she wanted you to have".

Henrietta's hands are trembling as she struggles to open the sealed envelope. She finally succeeds in opening it and takes the cheque out and reads it. She suddenly clutches her head with both hands; her eyes pop out and her jaws drop and she screams. "Unbelievable! Are you sure all these are for me?"

"Certainly, they are for you, my dear". Says Mr Dickenson.

"Obviously no one would have believed she was that well-off". Says Mr Foster.

"She mentioned that she last saw you on a beach in Australia when you were about five years old and was very fond of you". Says Barrister John Jones.

"We have been trying to find you since her death, we went through the voter's register and marriage registers throughout Europe and the US, and Australia. We were able to find you because of your marriage a few days ago; your name appeared in the marriage register and we were contacted immediately". Says Mr Dickenson.

Henrietta, pointedly at Morris, "My husband is the only person she had, he helped her enormously till her demise.

Barrister John Jones presents Henrietta with a document to sign, which she quickly signs and gives back to him. Mr Dickenson and Mr Foster counter sign and all three men leave the house, closing the door behind them.

Morris remains indifferent through out the episode. Henrietta goes to Morris and hugs him and says, "A few minutes ago you were saying that we should move to a different neighbourhood. Right now I can assure you that we can afford to buy a house anywhere in the world. I did not know that Nan was that rich."

"There you are," says Morris, "never judge a book by its cover."

Henrietta continues, "We have to buy a bigger house now, since you have got a lot of friends, don't you think?"

"It does not matter really whether we live in a large house or a small one, definitely not the kind of house that may alienate one from one's neighbours. We want to be a part of the community and play an active role within the community. We need to spread Peace and Happiness". Says Morris, with emphasis.

The following day, Henrietta goes searching for a house to buy and sees an advertisement about a property in Poole, Dorset. She arranges to go and view it. She asks Morris to go with her and he obliges to go along with it.

A few days later, on the day of the appointment, they drive to Dorset to meet the estate agent who advertised the property. They are in the office of the estate agent drinking coffee served to them when an elderly couple came in. The estate agent introduces the elderly couple to Morris and Henrietta as Mr and Mrs Boardman, the owners of the property they are going to view.

Mr Boardman Thanks Morris and Henrietta for coming all the way from London to view the property, and says, "My wife and I, have a lot of good memories in the house but we moved to Spain eighteen months ago because the weather in the UK is no longer conducive for us in our old age".

"We were going to leave the house to our son but he disappeared, we have no idea where he is". Says Mrs Boardman.

"Did you say he disappeared?" Asks Henrietta.

"Yes", replies Mrs Boardman, "he used to stay away all night and only came home very early in the mornings, and one morning, he did not come back. It's been a couple of years since and we've had no contact whatsoever". She turns to Mr Boardman and says "It's your fault for buying him that guitar on his sixteenth birthday, he changed a lot after that.

"He is not our flesh and blood, if you get my drift." Says Mr Boardman.

"What do you mean by that?" Asks Morris.

"We adopted him when he was eight years old says Mrs Boardman. And we treated him like our own, obviously we made a mistake as it turns out.

"What is his name?" Asks Morris.

"Isabbul". Replies Mr Boardman.

"<u>Who?</u>" Morris and Henrietta ask at the same time with shock and bewilderment.

Henrietta turns to Morris and asks, "Is life one big circle or what?"

"You tell me. Is it?" Morris Asks.